Christmas Murder at Eve Manor

Martin Hooper

Contents

CHAPTER 1 - 22ND OF DECEMBER

George Lawrence stumbled up the wooden stairs, stopping arms laden, on the top step. He breathed heavily, his warm breath colliding with the cold air, creating a cloud in front of him. He slowly maneuvered the axe wedged under his armpit to the floor and it dropped with a clunk, freeing up his arm to then pull a wood basket closer to himself before offloading the weight in his arms. He wheezed again and held his hand against the wall of his hut; he wouldn't ever admit it to anyone else but this afternoon's work has been hard going. Whereas a stubborn rebuttal greeted anyone who suggested that his age may be catching up with him, he had no doubts that each day brought new aches, pains, and lethargy. He could remember proudly reaching forty and waking each day with the same vigour and work ethic as when he was in his twenties, it flew directly in the face of the guys who used to warn him that when he reached their age he wouldn't be able to hack it the same, but he had. The same feeling when he reached fifty yet the last decade and finally hitting sixty had led to his physical body failing to match the enthusiasm he still had in his mind. He regularly woke with aches and pains, stiff hips and lower back, longing for bed earlier in the evening, and as he had noticed today, a capitulation of his lungs after any physical exertion. He pushed against his arm leaning against the hut and forced himself to quickly tidy before finishing outside. He leant over and grabbed the axe he had dropped to the floor, using it as a crutch. With one foot his pushed the basket full of logs under a small shelter which kept the majority of the wood in dry condition. He turned and stepped back down the steps before looking out across the view, a crisp blanket of snow covered the ground, trees, and small holly bush he had to the side of the hut. He had heard somewhere that Holly bushes to the side of a door was meant to ward off witches or evil spirits, he couldn't remember which side of the door the holly bush was supposed to stand in order for its magic to work but there it sat to the left of the hut, glistening under the wetness of snow which covered the small enclaves of each leaf, surely no yuletide Christmas cards could beat the imagery which sat directly in his eye line. He stepped off the bottom step and his foot crunched satisfyingly in the unbroken snow. His large footprints littered the surrounding landscape, somewhat defacing the tranquillity of the snow covered ground but even so he enjoyed the satisfaction of creating new footprints in the snow and purposefully aimed for the crisp unfettered surface of crystalised rainfall with each step. The axe firmly in hand despite its bulky head, he trotted around the back of the hut to place it back into the small shed. The small window from the hut hung above the small shed and the light shining out of was welcoming and warm, it was only upon seeing the contrast of the light did he realize how dark it had gotten. It was the 22nd of December so Winter Solstice has just passed so by all accounts the long road to summer had started, would be a while before he noticed the longer days plus the worst of the winter weather was yet to come but still it cheered him. It was clearly dark now but as ever with cold crisp evenings, the moon bounced off the snow creating a natural light that would have allowed George to carry on working if he had so wanted or still had the energy. Still that small window and the warm light that teased out from inside the hut was enticing. He placed the axe in the small shed balanced against the numerous tools and discarded garden objects and pushed the small wooden door closed. It dragged in the snow but he pushed it shut until it clicked closed, before he turned and headed back towards the hut entrance. He got to the front of the hut and stopped, lifting one foot in the air ready to stub his boot against the step to remove the snow clinging to his foot. His foot pulled backwards ready to kick it to remove the snow paused prior to kicking. He thought he had heard the unmistakable crunch of a foot compressing snow.

'Hello?' He called out. He heard no response and gave the step a thump with his foot, the snow sliding across the step and off his boot. He had no doubt heard something, and would have guessed it to have been a foot pressing down in the snow but none of the hotel staff would have come down here which ruled them out. Patricia was the only person who would ever want to speak to him and she would never have trudged through the snow to come see him unexpected. If the offer of a sleigh and reindeer to make the journey to the hut had been made she would have refused due to the cold. None of the other staff would have bothered; they neither cared for him nor the job enough to walk down here, snow or no snow. Brian the cook would have complained of an inability to leave his kitchen unattended, despite a lack of any guests, and had never shown any inclination that he courted friendship from George. George in fact knew little about him; he had arrived with such glowing reverence from Patricia and seemed to agree with her opinion of himself. George knew little about culinary skills nor could he understand the high regard with which modern chefs around the globe held themselves. Food was food plain and simple, and it could be judged as bad food or good food. He had no idea why some people forked out huge amounts of money for delicacies the size of acorns with a drizzle of sauce when a far more hearty meal could be plucked from any store shelf. Anyway, Brian appeared to regard himself as the next culinary messiah and for some reason this went hand in hand with conceitedness. George often wondered whether Brian's personality had drawn him to the profession or the profession had moulded him, he leaned towards the latter in the presence of Patricia who inflated Brian's ego whenever she was with him. The demonstrations of praise however had died away a little across the two months on the lead up to Christmas as Brian's presence at the Hotel had failed to garner the level of bookings for Christmas as had been hoped. His ego didn't seem to notice but George had felt that Patricia's sycophancy had been less forthcoming lately. That being said the staff Christmas meal which Brian prepared had been superb, which made George ponder why Brian did not use his talent to improve dishes such as Christmas dinners rather than conjuring up ridiculous food works of art.

Nonetheless, neither Brian nor Patricia would have graced the hut which was right at the bottom of the grounds of the hotel and out of sight; George doubted if they even remembered he existed. Joe the receptionist and Katie, who seemed to do everything across the hotel, were far more amenable and the only reason George had called out. Both were young and friendly and George was always pleasantly surprised at how nicely they spoke to him whenever he saw them at the hotel. That being said anyone working at the hotel could have contacted him via the telephone link in the hut so there was no conceivable reason why any one of them would journey down here. They had all come down once, apart from Brian, usually as part of their induction of joining the staff. In fact, Katie had wandered down once because she said the phone connection wasn't working but George reckoned she had wanted to walk down to blow off some steam. He remembers her giving snippets of a grievance she was having, almost waiting for his approval that she should continue, before they spent the walk up the hotel with Katie berating the poor work ethic of all those involved at the hotel. This was prior to Joe joining, and Katie seemed to approve of his attitude to helping her run the place. They were both the same age, and good looking as far as George could gather but he didn't believe that any romance had blossomed, more an appreciation of each other. He kicked his other boot against the step and trudged up the steps and into the warmth of the hut, closing the door behind himself. The door closed and the silence of the crisp winter's evening again engulfed the landscape and the hut. Silence apart from the crunch of footsteps walking slowly towards the hut.

George slipped off his coat and hung it on a small hook on the wall and small bits of snow fell to the floor as he slipped of his boots. The hut was warm, and welcoming, the lights were bright and not as cosy as one would think of a small hut in a snow laden landscape but the hut served more than one purpose. It was also the hotels security base. George could not work out why the hotel needed a security hut, but a combination of the hut being out of use, Patricia's overblown security fears, and it was another feature which the hotel could publish on their advertising materials. The hut had been purchased as part of the building originally, and stood vacant for a long time, when George has started working, he used it frequently just for keeping tools. It had helped that he had discovered that the hut had a number of tools inside which were in fine condition. However as Patricia sought to upgrade her clientele and the market of the hotel, she decided to make it into a gardening outpost plus security centre. The name was far more extravagant that what the hut actually entailed but it did link up to a few security cameras across the grounds of the hotel, mainly where guests could park their cars and above the main reception. It also had a telephone line through to the hotel but aside from that was rather basic in functionality. However the inside looked glossy and bright and they had taken a number of photos for the hotel webpage to exemplify why guests security was paramount throughout their stay. George always thought this was a strange selling technique as security generally represents threat, but apparently it had been popular with guests according to Patricia. This would probably be less so if any of the guests realized George was in charge of the hut, rarely inside it, as to him it was still there for gardening, and that he didn't care whether the guests' valuables were stolen. In fact he would be surprised if any such crime ever did occur on the premises as it never had done before. One of the old receptionists had lifted petty cash from the restaurant till but that was the single offense George could recall in all his time there. He couldn't remember the receptionist's name and they were gone shortly after. Surely the hotel would have done better to promote 'The hotel which has never had a crime, we don't even need security!' He lumbered down and sat down in his chair, he would be leaving soon so there was no point making himself comfortable aside from removing his coat and boots. He could have left there and then without anyone noticing but he hadn't ever made a habit of leaving early so he wasn't going to start today, even if it was his last day before Christmas. The hotel was closed between 23rd until 27th of December, Patricia was having some guests but they were friends and family as far as George could recall and she had decided to tend to them personally. He couldn't imagine

Patricia changing beds nor making breakfasts and he had been proven partly correct when he found that Brian, Joe, and Katie were all staying until Christmas Eve. He however was not needed, he had filled all the log baskets with dry wood and done everything that could have been done in the garden and thus was surplus to requirements. He was absolutely fine with that, he enjoyed working but he enjoyed the festive period more. The food, the alcohol, family, the festivities, he loved it all, and four days away from the hotel was the perfect break. He'd had little in terms of a send-off, they had had a staff Christmas meal, but none of the staff had called through today to wish him a Merry Christmas. He didn't think Patricia was the type but he thought as his boss she would have taken the courtesy of a twenty second phone call.

He sat back and flicked his eyes across the three monitors, not a single movement on any of the screens and he cast his eyes back up to the hut window. It was pitch black outside despite the snow; the clouds must have covered the light from the moon. He flicked on the light which lights up the outside of the hut and it illuminated across the snow, no doubt the hotel could have seen the glow over the small hill coming from the hut's outside light. He lent back and rubbed his hand through his hair on the back of his head, he was tired but what a lovely feeling, he felt like he had earned his break today. He rubbed his eyes and stood up, the chair creaking as his weight lifted upwards and eased the pressure on the chair. He moved to the window and looked out; he was working out whether he should wander up to the hotel and say merry Christmas to everyone before going or just leave? They hadn't shown him the same courtesy but the internal battle of wanting to share a little Christmas cheer was getting the better of him. He had just about finished so a ten minute walk up to the hotel could count as the end of his shift. He glanced down at the shed door as he turned but then turned his head back. The door was open. He knew he had heard someone outside and cursed himself for second guessing himself.

'God dammit!' He grabbed his coat off the hook and slid it over his arm as he pushed one of his feet into his boot, some of the snow had melted in the warmth but he had only been inside a few minutes so much of the snow on his boots and coat fell onto the floor of the hut. He hadn't even stopped to ponder whether there was a reasonable explanation or a crazed maniac was outside, he was fuming at the fact he had ignored the feeling he had that someone was outside. He slipped on his other boot and opened the door and stepped outside, the night was so crisp and still, the crystalised snow was reflecting small twinkles back to George from the reflection of the light from around the side of the hut. He closed the door and stepped on the first step and stopped. He had hurried so quick to get outside that he hadn't really stopped to think, a real chill spread through his body now he had closed the door. Everything was so still and quiet, he knew he had closed the shed door because of it sticking in the snow. What if it was someone stealing tools and they were still here? The thought of that axe popped into George's mind. He shook his head to himself, whatever the explanation, it wasn't his problem, if there had been a burglary, he would report it and go home. He was outside now so he may as well walk round and see what was what. He trudged back round the side of the hut, the compressed snow squeaking under his boots. He got to the shed door, there were footprints around it but he had been in and out so no more than he would normally see. For a second he was puzzled as to why he was worried, obviously he had left the shed door open but then as he peered inside and noticed the axe was missing, he was now certain someone else had left the shed ajar. He pulled the shed door further open as it pushed against the snow, leaving a snow angel like flattening of the snow it cleared. It was only the axe which was absent. At first he feared the ramifications of the axe being the only tool taken; if it was a simple robbery then it was far from the most prized tool in the shed. Then he came to his senses, why else would someone take an axe? It was Christmas after all and there was a small block of pine trees not far from the hotel. How tiresome, he found it incredibly unlikely that whoever took the axe was likely to replace it, especially after having to drag a tree to wherever it was intended. The best he could do was look out and about at front windows for any freshly cut looking pine trees which he hadn't noticed in the last week. Even then how was he supposed to confront or prove that it was them that had removed his axe, more likely than anything, it was the last he would see of the axe. He looked up at the bright light shining directly down from the hut and the small window below it which now seemed dark against the contrast of the bright security light. He stood there whilst he tried to consider whether he should mention the axe now or after his break, it would only delay his getaway this evening, and he could even say it was taken whilst he was off which was probably the easiest solution. Then again, it may have been returned to the shed by the time he got back. He kept he eyes on the small hut window, he was struggling to see as the brightness from the security light bulb was blinding him but as he squinted, he thought the hut window was darker and more obscured than it should be. He kept staring despite the fact that when he blinked or looked away, the positive afterimage of the bulb glowed. He squeezed his eyes and then squinted again, the shape which was blocking the window moved, and in a flash was gone. There was somebody in the hut. He swirled round to make back towards the front door.

'Oh no you don't you little...' he bumbled forward despite the fact that the afterimage from staring at the bulb was still hovering in his eye line. He jogged round to the front, he had no doubts about it now, it was a group of kids messing around, whilst he had given up on the axe if it had been put to use for Christmas tree felling, it was another matter if some youths had stolen it. If he left now, he couldn't even imagine what state the hut would be in when he got back. He got back to the door, and he hadn't heard anyone leave nor did he think they could have been quick enough without him glancing a look at them, so more than likely they were inside. He knew better than to corner any kind of animal but George didn't want to hurt them in any way, just wanted to scare them a little. He could remember a glare he received from a distance from a local farmer when he was younger. He had been knocking dry stone wall stones down a hill and watching them pick up speed and clatter at the bottom when a farmer had yelled out at him and he took off running. He had turned to see the farmer at a distance glaring at him and they had made eye contact, and it had filled his heart with fear. He stayed indoors for the next two weeks through pure terror he would be reprimanded the second he was spotted outside his home. George stood outside the door, he knew the fear of being caught was far worse than anything George could muster so he prolonged the wait, half expecting the child to zip past him the second he opened the door. He opened the shed door, with a stern face but it quickly dropped to a face of confusion as he was met by an empty hut. He stepped inside and realized that there was definitely nobody inside, he'd missed him. He looked around the desk, nothing had been taken as far as he could tell and he glanced at his watch, it was the end of his shift before Christmas and no harm had been done so he decided to just leave the hut. He quickly moved around the room flicking off the different screens, he should have probably shut everything down completely to save energy as he was not going to be back until after Christmas but he wasn't exactly sure if all the cameras carried on working when it was all switched off completely. Anyhow he wasn't paying the bills nor was the security his idea. He quickly glanced around the room and turned towards the door, pulling it open, the chill from outside gusted in to the room and gave him a chill as he reached around the back of the door to flick off the light switch to the hut. As the lights flicked off and the bulb ceased to illuminate the room, the small window still gave a ray of brightness from the moon shining into the room. The ray of moonlight shone across the room, illuminating the shape of a figure rising silently from beneath the bank of screens which were now off but their small standby lights continued to glow warmly. The figure rose to stand, and the moonlight illuminated the glint of the sharpened axe in the figure's hands. George moved forward and grabbed the door handle to pull the door behind him but fell forward stumbling down the shed stairs. He felt like he had been hit by a train in his back, pushing him forward flat into the snow. The pain still had not hit him, and he tried to turn his neck to see what had pushed him with such force down the stairs, but as he moved to turn his head the pain in his upper back screamed at him and he was unable to move to turn. His forehead pressed against the snow and as he tried to push his head up but his body was no longer responding to his commands. He slumped down and the taste of metallic blood filled his mouth and contrasted with the cold snow pressed against his cheek. He could feel beads of sweat pouring down his face and he tried to move his arm forward to push himself onto his back but he only managed to crawl his fingers in the cold snow. His legs kicked but to no avail as he writhed into the snow on the floor, he listened as the slow steps out of the hut moved steadily closer and began a slow methodical descent of the steps. He tried again to use his arm to push himself over so he could try and understand what had happened but the pain in his back crippled his attempts and his face again slumped into the snow.

'My teacher said I never should…' a raspy voice broke the silence of the night and broke George's feeling of adrenaline as the pain in his back increased.

'Talk to strangers in the wood…' The voice was menacing, angry, and arrogant at the same time. George could tell from the way the words were slowly delivered that they anger was directed at him. He tried to speak but only managed in coughing into the snow.

'If I did she would say…' George felt the presence of the figure above him but his peripheral vision was unable to make out anything of the figure but he knew the person was stood directly above him. He felt immense pain in his upper back, and the sound of his own grinding flesh as the axe was released from his back. His right eye was pressed against the snow, with the sweat from his forehead and snow blurring his vision. He wanted to turn or to pull himself up and away but his body felt numb, not answering to his will. In what felt like an eternity of silence, George felt as if he had been left alone, the calmness of the surroundings again making itself clear, his right shoulder burned and he winced as he tried to move as it forced the weight of his body onto his shoulder. He thought if he could pull himself towards the hut and call for help, then he might be ok.

'Naughty boy to disobey' The final words trickled out and George realized that his plan was not going to come to fruition. His eyes rolled upwards to try and look forward, the sharp prickles of the holly bush leaves glistening in the still cold night. He noticed the gentle fall of snowflakes against his cheek. *It's snowing* he thought to himself before the thud of the axe came down again.

CHAPTER 2 - 23RD OF DECEMBER

'This is bloody brilliant!' Robbie said, slouched back in his passenger seat as he watched the village streets roll past the car window. 'I mean what more could you want? We have a quintessential English village, it's nearly Christmas, we're off to a grand hotel with free food and drinks, and to top it off, its blooming snowing!' He looked over anticipatorily at Eric, who did not respond to him, his full concentration on navigating the roads ahead of him. The wipers were moving quickly to clear the snow but no other cars were on the ever increasing snow covered road.

'Yeah well I'll be happier once we actually arrive, this snow is mental!' He leaned forward in his seat as if trying to look further into the distance.

'I don't know why you're so worried, worst case scenario, we find ourselves a traditional pub, the kind of one with a grumpy barmen and roaring fire, and we drink until the snow clears.' Robbie smiled to himself, relaxing back in his chair. He then leaned forward and flicked the radio on, the song of Christmas pop songs filled the car.

'Don't Robbie, I need to concentrate', Eric flicked the radio back off nonchalantly and resumed staring straight forward into the snow. Robbie stared at him for a second.

'You joking? What difference does the radio make? There are no other cars on the road anyway. And Mr Grinch, its Wham, who says no to *Last Christmas* the day before Christmas Eve?' He resisted the urge to put the radio back on but he was itching to push Eric.

'Anyway, I thought you said this was the village, you said it was it was like a fifteen minute drive from here?'

'It is, but no cars, let alone any salt spreaders have touched these roads, so I'm taking it easy. I don't think I have ever seen snow like this before either, not exactly ideal driving conditions'. The car trundled along in the snow slowly decreasing as Eric strained to work out which side of the road he was on, was it not for the short hedges which ran along the ride side of the road, he could have easily been driving across an open field for all he knew. He kept looking out of his window, attempting to work out recognizable shapes from the snow covered landscapes but beyond a blanket of white he was not entirely sure where he was or if he was heading in the right direction. His car was hardly roadworthy let alone with the extravagances of satnavs and warming seats so apart from the rough general direction he was attempting the route from memory. Problem was that this memory was a hazy memory from years of being driven by his parents to the hotel, and he had never encountered the roads covered in snow.

'So fill me in' Robbie cut into his concentration on the road, 'who is to be joining us at the manor for our Christmas festivities? And do I have to make small talk or am I free to enjoy the amenities in peace?'

'I reckon we can keep ourselves to ourselves. I mean I'll have to be nice to my aunt because she's letting us stay etc. and I think she sees it as a family gathering of some sort, apart from that I don't know. I think I'm the only family member going' Eric glanced over at Robbie and then back to the road.

'What's she like? Your aunt?' Robbie stayed laid back in his car seat.

'Great aunt actually, she's mum's aunt, and she's alright. Can be a little scary but she's got a heart of gold'

'What do you mean scary?' Robbie's eyebrows rose with a quizzical look.

'Not scary scary but she used to be a headmistress at a school, so she has that stereotypical school teacher demeanour, you know, prim and proper, a bit like McGonagall in Harry Potter' Eric glanced over 'she's fine, just I can see why some people would find her strict'.

'Whatever, I'll charm her, and then I'll enjoy her alcohol' He smiled to himself and looked out ahead onto the road. He sat forward with a jolt and quickly turned his head straining to see behind the car.

'What did you say the name of the hotel was?' turning his neck back to Eric.

'Eve Manor, why?'

‘Stop the car matey, sure I’ve just seen a sign pointing to the right.’
Eric looked at him and then turned his neck, trying to see the sign which Robbie had claimed to have seen.
‘Can’t be, there’s no turn in the road, we can’t have missed it, it must just be further on.’ Eric continued slowly moving.
‘Mate, I just seen the bloody sign, honestly, just stop the car and I’ll show you.’ He gestured with his hands that the sign was behind them. Eric looked at him and the car rolled to a stop.
‘What if I can’t get him moving again?’ Eric said worryingly looking at the road ahead and the snow.
‘Who cares? You’ve stopped it now anyway, go check out that sign and you’ll know I was right.’ Eric stared at Robbie disbelievingly.
‘What do you mean? Why I am checking it out?’ He turned in his chair to look at Robbie.
‘I haven’t a clue where we are going, so I wouldn’t able to confirm or deny anyway.’
Eric didn’t say anything in reply, he unclipped his seatbelt, the material of the belt zipping across his coat and buckling back in its holder. He clicked open the door, and twisted his body so both feet trod into the snow, it was already far past his ankles on the road, and

looked knee deep on the banks of the road. He pulled himself out the car and stood up, closing the car door behind him. He raised a hand to his eyes as the snow was still falling quickly and it was sticking to his eyelashes, he trudged to the back of the car, attempting to see what Robbie had seen but could see nothing which resembled a sign. He followed the compressed snow where the car had been which was already becoming freshly covered in fresh snow. He watched the snow falling for a moment and quickly came to the realization that time really was of the essence, he wasn't sure if he would get much further in this weather. He stepped round the passenger side and pulled the car door open.

'Out' he demonstrated the motion with his hand.

'Jesussssssss' Robbie hurled away from the cold and snow, in a manner reminiscent of Christopher Lee recoiling from the light.

'Come on, I can't see anything, plus the road is pretty bad so we best be quick' Eric again motioned for Robbie to step out the car. 'Up, up, up!' Robbie unbuckled his belt and jumped out the car quickly, pushing past Eric, he quickly pranced past the back of the car, his feet bopping in and out of the snow like he was treading on hot coals and into the whirl of snow. Eric pushed the door closed and followed after him, almost tracing his footprints in the snow. About 20 metres back, he could see Robbie, stood facing him, arms out as if presenting a new car to a TV contestant.

'What did I tell you? Eve Manor Hotel, turn right here.' He looked triumphantly at Eric, who was still trudging forward to examine what Robbie was presenting to him. He stood next to Robbie and could see where he had wiped the snow from the sign; the italic large blue font from the sign confirmed what Robbie had told him.

'Thank you!' Robbie chimed in with an air triumph.

'Whatever.' Eric ignored the happiness which was filling Robbie's face, 'it doesn't make sense anyway, there isn't a right turn here, that's obviously why I didn't notice it or pay attention.'

'That's where you're wrong again Sherlock' Robbie redirected his outstretched arms to his right, 'Welcome to Eve Manor Hotel'. Eric followed the direction of Robbie's arms and beneath a snow covered tree which was hanging with the weight of the snow, was a small sign.

'The roads completed covered' Eric trudged towards the sign; 'there's no way I can drive up there!' He trudged across the road to have a better look at the sign but his legs dragged with each step.

‘What? So what now? We can’t miss out!’ Robbie protested as he followed Eric to examine the road. ‘We’ve come too far, and I’m hungry to be honest’ He pushed his way through the snow, ‘look it’s not *that* bad, maybe if we take it the slow, the car will be fine?’ Eric shot Robbie a look which made clear his feelings on the idea. ‘Fine, well we’ll just walk it?’

‘Rob, it’s like 4 miles, and that’s just me hazarding a guess from what I remember, it could be a lot more, and in this snow it’ll take us ages. Not a chance’ Eric stood in the midst of thought.

‘Well, we haven’t exactly got a choice, we aren’t going to get far in the car, and I am sure as hell not spending the night in there, it’ll be like a freezer. Plus I have been promised roaring fires, booze and food over Christmas. I’m not been discovered on Boxing day, frozen in an embrace with you, in your piece of junk car.’ As much as Eric was inclined to disagree, Robbie had a point, the car wasn’t going to get much further and it was still snowing heavily, the chances of anyone using this road over the Christmas period, let alone gritting trucks was inconceivable. The odds of them spending all of Christmas sat in his car were a real possibility. ‘Come on buddy, the thought of a warm drink in front of the fire makes it worth it. And what a way to start our Christmas break! A festive walk through the snow. What you think??' Robbie's right, Eric thought, it was their only option, and the walk wouldn't be so bad knowing they had warm beds and fires waiting for them at his aunts. He nodded and trudged back through the snow towards the car, Robbie smiling and fist bumping behind him before jogging back to the car through the ever increasing snow.

It was dark by the time Robbie and Eric wearily approached Eve Manor, the day had drawn to a close, with the light hours of light blocked out by the snow filled clouds. The snow had eased up but not stopped altogether and the sky suggested more was to come before the end of the day. Both Robbie and Eric's face glistened with sweat, they had not rushed the ascending path to Eve Manor but the snow was almost waist height by the time they had got around halfway. From then on, each step involved dragging the leg through the snow, and then pushing it forward through the compacted deep snow. The snow surrounding the manor was far less deep, a combination of footsteps seemed to have downtrodden the area immediately around the front entrance, but even along the drive in front the snow was only around ankle deep. Eric could see cars alongside of the building which were pretty much covered by snow but anyone looking immediately outside the front entrance would not have conceived the banks of snow which had all but cut off the outside world.

'Never again mate, that was brutal.' Robbie panted out his words as he rolled a medium sized rucksack from his bag onto the floor. Eric, walked past him, tapping Robbie on the back as Robbie stood hands on knees panting.

'Come on mate, wasn't so bad, let's get a well-earned beer' Eric smiled and approached the door; Robbie looked up and smiled and grab the strap of his rucksack swinging it alongside him as he followed him to the door. Eric gave a wrap at the door, despite the twists of modern technology which the hotel had incorporated; the building still retained a classical old style, its large frame doors and large bay windows looking out from the hotel. They could hear the approaching of mumbled voices behind the door, and their shoes squeaked on the compressed snow as the door opened, shining a warm glow across the rapidly darkening afternoon.

‘Eric! Ohhh’ the lady who had answered the door lurched forward and hugged Eric warmly.

‘Hello Auntie Pat’ Eric mumbled over the shoulder of his aunt as she squeezed him tight.

‘You’re freezing! Come on in! Please don’t tell me you have been out in this terrible weather for long? Where on earth is your car?’ She glanced across from Eric as she relinquished the hug, ‘whom do we have here?’ a chillier tone emanated from Patricia as she looked Robbie up and down.

‘This is Robbie, he’s alone this Christmas so thought it would be nice for him to come along, the more the merrier.’ Eric looked from his aunt to Robbie and then back to his aunt seeking any inclinations of approval.

‘It’s a pleasure and thank you’ Robbie beamed a smile at Patricia.

‘Indeed.’ Patricia continued to look at Robbie, and the hint of a grimace cross her face, ‘the more the merrier.’ She looked back to Eric, ‘well come on in, we can’t stay out here all night’. She ushered them both in with a wave of the arm and moved into the hotel. The warmth greeted the two like a warm towel as they stepped inside of the hotel. Robbie tugged at Eric’s arm.

‘You didn’t mention I was coming?’ he whispered so that Patricia would not overhear.

‘It’s fine, anyway we’re here now, why are you bothered?’ He looked back at Robbie.

‘Well I suppose I don’t really care but a little forewarning would have been nice’ He let go of Eric’s arm and they continued to follow Eric’s aunt as they approached a reception room, with the main desk reception at the front.

‘We’re closed at the moment so not everything is working as it would normally but we still have a few staff of who will be staying until tomorrow. I presume you don’t mind anyway?’ Patricia looked at the two men.

‘Of course not, we’re grateful for a bed and the invite’ Robbie said quickly, looking for approval from the taut face of Patricia.

‘The invitation was not extended but you will both receive a warm bed throughout your stay.’ She said coldly. ‘Regarding rooms, we have plenty of free rooms, are you looking…’ Patricia stumbled over the words, ‘…are you requiring a shared room?’ She looked at the two men with a hint of disapproval.

‘We would be grateful for whatever you can…’ Robbie started, continuing his over indulgent attempt at ingratiating himself to Patricia.

‘Auntie, we’re not a couple!’ Eric cut in, ‘I used to be married.’

‘Well you never know nowadays, especially with these younger generations, you all seem to swap beds and sexual partners with such frequency. I was merely trying to be accommodating.’ She appeared to relax in her manner and half smiled towards Robbie. ‘I’ll call Katie or Joe to come show you to your rooms.’ She pressed a small button by reaching behind the reception desk, and with seconds a young female had appeared from behind the door at the reception desk, she beamed a smile at all three. ‘Katie, could you possibly show these two to their rooms? We’ll have to open the room next to 16 as we have a guest we weren’t expecting; I assume the room is fine?’

‘Course I will and yes, 17 was cleaned yesterday with the rest of the rooms.’ She beamed a smile back and collected some keys from the drawer in front of her before beckoning Robbie and Eric to follow after her, ‘if you’ll please follow me, I’ll show you to your rooms. Would you like any help with your bags?’

‘We’re ok thanks’ Robbie answered as they followed after her.

‘Will see you down here shortly’ Patricia called after them, all three unclear as to whom see was referring, both Katie and Eric returning a nod in her direction. Robbie and Eric followed after Katie as she pushed through a double door leading to some stairs; she held the door open for them to both come through.

‘Don’t worry, its only one flight of stairs, we’re all staying on the first floor with there only being a few guests and the hotel being closed, I think Mrs Crabshaw thought it would be more cosy that way.’

‘Sounds lovely’ Robbie smiled at Katie as they started the stairs, ‘bit hard on you working though’.

‘You can just tell us the room number if you like and we’ll find it’ Eric agreed with Robbie.

‘No don’t worry honestly, it’s fairly quiet anyway, there is only the eleven of us including staff’ she turned to speak to them as they walked up the stairs ‘it’s a lot quieter that it usually is, so gives me something to do. It’ll be even quieter tomorrow when us staff leave, it’ll only be the eight of you.’

'You're leaving tomorrow?' Eric said a little dejectedly. Katie nodded and smiled back. 'You might be lucky. We had to dump the car on the road and walk up here' Eric continued.
'The snow is awful' Robbie added, 'you'd be better staying here' He smiled again at Katie but she didn't reciprocate.
'What? Really? I am supposed to meet my boyfriend tomorrow morning on the road so we can travel down to see his family over Christmas'. Robbie's smile stiffened on his face. They reached the top of the stairs and pushed another set of double doors leading to a long corridor with rooms adjacent on both sides of the corridor. The walls were tastefully decorated with trimmings of holly and ivy.
'I'm sorry, they were really bad when we left and it's still snowing now, unless somebody clears it, I'm not sure you'll be able to reach the road, let alone meet your boyfriend. Can't you call him?' Eric was sympathetic as he glanced at the door numbers as they walked past the rooms down the corridor.
'I'll have to I guess, there is no mobile reception here so I haven't had any updates from the outside world. I will let him know about the weather, maybe it'll clear up overnight. Knowing my luck, Mrs Bradshaw will have me working all the way through Christmas.' She

stopped in front of a door with the number 16. 'Anyway, here are your rooms, 17 is just next door to it.' She smiled again, her face returning to its usual upbeat appearance. 'I best go make some phone calls I guess, let me know if you want anything'.

'We will' Eric said and smiled. She nodded and turned.

'Sorry about the snow!' Robbie called after her, taking one of the keys off Eric. Katie glanced back and smiled before disappearing back through the double doors from which they had come. 'She seems nice' Robbie turned to Eric smiling. Eric looked at Robbie but said nothing, turning back to his door and turning the key in the doorknob, and then turning back to Robbie who was still stood staring at him.

'You not going to your room?' Eric asked.

'Na, just going to drop my stuff in your room.' Robbie looked blankly back at Eric.

'Why are you dropping your stuff in my room, your room is all of 5 feet away?' he motioned towards the corresponding door with his head, as he pushed his room door open.

'Don't be daft, we can just drop our stuff and go straight down and get a drink', Robbie pushed passed a nonplussed Eric and into his

room, 'no need to get comfy, what we need is a stiff beverage'.
Robbie smiled and dropped his bag inside the room. 'Hey this isn't bad.' He looked around the modern decorated room, which defied the buildings older exterior, 'anyway come on.' He pushed back past Eric and nodded with his head. Eric shimmied his bag off his shoulder, onto the floor next to Robbie's strewn bag and proceeded to close and lock the door. They headed back down the corridor from where they had come, Robbie pushing open the door to the stairs and motioning for Eric to go first. The sound of whispered but animated voices greeted them coming up the stairs.
'This is ridiculous, we can just head home now, the woman is intolerable!' the whispered voice of a man drifted up from down the flight of stairs.
'Michael just grow up! You've got the patience of a 4 year old.' A woman's voice in a calmer whispered tone replied, 'let's go get a drink and make the most of it'.
'I don't want to sit and listen to excruciating small talk, it's just about...' He was cut off as he glanced up and saw Eric and Robbie heading down the stairs, he cheeks reddened.

'Evening' Eric smiled as they pushed past the two stood just inside the stairwell. Robbie followed with a slight nod to the lady.

'Evening' she beamed back as Eric and Robbie walked through the door, leaving the two stood in the stairwell.

'That sounded heated' Robbie said as they got a few strides way.

'Blimey, you want everyone to hear?' Eric said in shocked reply.

'Doesn't matter, just stating the obvious, who are they anyway?'

'Never seen them before in my life' Eric said.

'Eh? I thought the place was closed and it was just family and a few staff' Robbie look puzzled.

'So did I, but you heard them, maybe they are the last of the guests and heading home today?' Robbie seemed happy at this suggestion and shrugged his shoulders. They walked up to the reception desk where they had been greeted by Katie previously, it was vacant again.

'Blimey, you can't get the staff nowadays.' Robbie said, leaning his arm on the reception and smiling at Eric.

'How can I help?' A voice appeared from behind reception causing Robbie to jump back in surprise.

'Crap! You gave me a jump then mate!' Robbie said as he looked at the young man stood at reception where there had previously been nobody 'you hiding back there?' The young man smiled back politely.

'I was just organizing under the desk, I finish tomorrow, so want to make sure everything is in order for when I return' He continued to smile looking from Robbie, to Eric, and then back to Robbie.

'Not sure you'll be getting far.' Eric looked towards the windows; the snowing drifted down past the pane was not a true reflection of the weather he had recently trudged through. The young man inclined his head with a puzzled look towards Robbie following the comment.

'Never mind him, where can we rustle up a drink?' Robbie said.

'There is an assortment of drinks in the lounge where the rest of the guests are which Mrs Bradshaw asked to be provided but if they are not to your liking, please do come and let me know.' The young man continued looking at Robbie and Eric obviously looking for confirmation that their exchange had finished.

'Perfect, thank you' Eric said, the young man gave a nod, Robbie gave a small salute to no response from the young man who continued to stand to attention as Robbie and Eric turned away and headed towards the direction of the lounge.

‘Blimey, I didn’t realize your Auntie had staffed the place with robots.’ Robbie said as they across the lobby away from the desk.

‘He was a little rigid, why’d you not tell him about the weather?’ Eric asked.

‘I wanted a drink, and after the way you blabbed about the terrible weather to that girl upstairs and how she rushed off, I didn’t want you scaring him away and me out of a drink. Why are you Mr Weather all of a sudden anyway?’ Eric gave Robbie a nonchalant shrug in response just as Katie walked through one of the doors by the reception and the two of them turned around.

‘Joe, are you going to spend the whole of today crouching behind that desk? You haven’t actually greeted any of the guests’ She said as she walked quickly past the desk. The young man in response raised his arm, and outstretched a palm in the direction of Robbie and Eric. Katie’s gaze moved away from Joe and in their direction, ‘Were your rooms ok?’ she said beaming a smile at them both. ‘You off to see the rest of the guests?’

'We are and the rooms were lovely thank you' Robbie said. Eric glared at him.

'Did you manage to get through to your boyfriend?' Eric enquired with sincerity.

'My..' Katie looked a little confused 'Ah my boyfriend, yes, sorry, yes I did. He is going to try and make the journey anyway and I will just do my best to meet him.' She smiled at Eric.

'You'll need skis' Robbie said. 'It's a lot worse out there than that drizzle floating past the windows'

'I'm sure we'll sort something out anyway' She smiled again, maybe with a hint of less enthusiasm. 'Anyway everyone is through there,' Katie point at a hard wood panelled door, the murmurs of voices could be heard.

'Thanks' Eric said.

'I'll see you both later, might even get time for a drink if everyone is going to be relaxing in there.' She smiled again as she walked off past the door and towards another, of which she disappeared through. Eric turned and stared at Robbie.

Eric turned and stared at Robbie. 'What was that skis comment for? I thought we weren't worrying the staff?'

'Na, that was before I knew where the drinks were. And besides, she would need skis, we struggled, and it has only carried on snowing since we got past the worst of it at the road.' Robbie replied. Eric knew he was right, there was very little chance anyone was leaving the hotel tomorrow unless the weather took a dramatic change. If anything, with the snow still falling, and the weather dropping as the night went on, the snow was bound to increase further.

'Well, let's make the most of this hotel shall we?' Eric smiled at Robbie.

'After you buddy' Robbie bowed and moved for Eric to approach the door. He pushed the door open the door and walked in. The room had a warm glow flicking from the open fire, and its décor seemed more suited to a stately home than the lounge of a hotel. There were large seats and one long sofa circling the fire which was the centre piece of the room, the panelled walls gave the room a dark feel but odd lamps scattered throughout the room added to the glow of the fire to create a warm cosy glow.

'Wow' Robbie said.

'Ahh Eric! Everyone, this is my niece's son Eric, he has delightfully agreed to spend the festive period with us' Patricia stood up and walked over, hooking Eric's arm. 'Is your room suitable?' she said directly to Eric.

'Yes it's wonderful, but this room is just...'

'Quite, it's the pride of the hotel, and perfect for these cold winter nights' Patricia said again addressing the room. 'Robert this is Barbara's son.' Patricia proudly brought Eric closer to the seated guests in the room. An older man, yet younger than Patricia stood up, his pot belly protruded as he stood, his buttons on his formal waistcoat pulling slightly as he eased himself up.

'Is he indeed?' the man ruffled in a low voice and offered his hand forward, which Eric shook, 'well we're family, in some distant manner.' Eric looked at the man with a puzzled smile 'don't worry, we have never met!' He turned to Patricia, 'look at the poor boy's face. Our family is too large! Patricia's husband Ralph was my father's brother.' He smiled to himself, 'complicated isn't it!'

'I'll say' Eric replied, relinquishing the handshake, 'but it's a pleasure to meet another member of the family'. Robert looked from Eric, passed him and at Robbie who had remained awkwardly behind Eric.

'Whom do we have here?'

‘Ah I neglected to say, partly as Eric failed to inform me, but he has brought a guest to join us for the festive period’ Patricia said. Robbie smiled and leaned his hand forward to shake the old man’s hand. Despite his younger looking appearance, the manner with which Robert acted betrayed his age, he almost seemed doddery.

‘Robbie. Nice to meet you.’

‘The more the merrier I say!’ Robert beamed. ‘How about I get you two fine gents a drink?’

‘A man after my own heart!’ Robbie laughed, the two walked towards a small table at the back of the room with an assortment of decanters and bottles of spirits laid out in splendour.

‘Eric dear, let me introduce you to another of the guests who will be spending Christmas with us.’ Patricia had pulled Eric’s arm despite his longing gaze towards the drinks. Hopefully Robbie has the courtesy to pour more than one drink, he thought to himself. Sat delicately on the end of the sofa close to the fire was a young blond lady. ‘Mrs Claypole is writing a blog about the hotel and its charm so make sure you behave if you don’t want your shenanigans across the web’ Patricia smiled.

‘Please call me Kailey’ the lady smiled at Eric, ‘and do not worry, I won’t be posted anything online about anybody’s behaviour, so please enjoy yourself.’ She had a smooth voice with a hint of a soft liverpudlian accent.

‘I wouldn’t have minded in the least, I just want a nice relaxed Christmas so I don’t think my behaviour would have been of any interest anyway. What’s your blog?’

‘Just an article about festive breaks and country hotels. I usually do travel writing but staying closer to home for winter and summer breaks has become more en vogue of late so here I am!’ she smiled again.

‘Well you’ve picked the right place.’ Patricia smiled and Kailey smiled back. Eric felt that the smile on the woman’s face was less than genuine and wasn’t entirely sure if Christmas spent with a few family members of a hotel proprietors was exactly what she had in mind. Essentially she would be working over Christmas. Robbie came round behind Eric and handed him a glass.

‘There you are old man, looking after you as always.’ He took a sip of his drink giving him a nod.

‘Robbie, this is Kailey, she’s spending Christmas here too.’ Robbie smiled at the lady sat on the sofa.

‘So are you family members who have met before? Or making acquaintances for the first time?’ Robbie enquired.

‘I don’t think we have any young ladies as pretty as Mrs Claypole in our family’ Robert had come up behind Robbie and stood next to him smiling at Kailey. He had also poured himself a large drink of what looked like whisky. Kailey smiled but did not say anything, Eric’s impression that she was not ecstatic about her stay with the family seemed to be confirmed as the smile faded and her eyes looked away almost searching for a way out of the situation.

‘Quite.’ Patricia glared at Robert.

He turned to look at Eric to avoid Patricia’s glare. ‘I hear from young Robbie that you had to abandon your car? Quite the expedition reaching the hotel was it?’ he said.

‘Not half.’ Robbie cut in, who took another sip of his drink. Eric noticed that it wouldn’t be long before he needed to top his drink up. ‘It’s really bad down the road, I don’t think anyone will be coming or going tomorrow unless you regularly have snow ploughs along the roads?’

‘Even if we did, they wouldn’t clear the road up to the hotel, especially this close to Christmas’ Patricia answered.

‘What about the staff?’ Eric asked, ‘aren’t they all finishing tomorrow?’

‘That is the plan but if the weather is as bad as you say, they’ll have no choice but to wait. We have more than enough rooms and food. Plus the finest chef in the region.’ She looked at Kailey who was oblivious to the comment as she gazed dreamily at the flickering fire.

‘They won’t be happy about that’ Robbie said, half to himself.

‘Well they have no choice, I can’t be blamed for the weather’ Patricia snapped back.

‘Well I think it’ll be splendid, the staff can come join us in here for Christmas day, and we’ll make the most of it!’ Robert grinned from ear to ear, ‘don’t you agree?’ He addressed the room without receiving any reply. He caught Kailey’s eye as she had looked up and she again gave him a weary smile.

‘Anyway, there is no point us all standing around, make yourselves comfortable’ Patricia ordered the guests. Robert returned to the chair where he had been sat when they came in. Robbie moved back towards the drinks at the back of the room in search of a top up to his glass, and Eric sat on the other end of the sofa. 'Right I will go and fetch Katie, and maybe we can think about getting some festive sandwiches brought in? How does that sound?' Patricia moved towards the door, shooting a disapproving glance at Robbie's freshly poured drink and back at him as he moved to sit by the fire. 'Not sure where the Foxs have got to, but I suppose I better ask if they would like some food too.' She half said aloud as she departed the room.

'Foxs?' Eric asked.

'Another couple staying at the hotel, they've brought their daughter too but I have hardly seen her, locked up in her room most the time.' Robert replied.

'Think we saw them on the stairs' Eric said.

'Arguing by the looks of it.' Robbie cut in, not averting his gaze from the fire which appeared to have captured the imagination of both Robbie and Kailey.

'Can't be having that, not at this time of year,' Robert said. The room fell to silence afterwards with the crack of the fire snapping occasionally.

'They've been arguing since they arrived.' Kailey broke the silence, all three men looking at the quiet woman by the fire, 'they were here yesterday before I arrived and I overheard them arguing then.'
'The guy seemed pretty intent on leaving when we overheard them.' Robbie said and looked to Eric.
'They're after the hotel I think.' Kailey said.
'The hotel?' Eric said. Robert moved uncomfortably in his chair. 'As in they want to own the hotel?' Kailey nodded in reply.
'Mrs Fox told me that they were staying over Christmas with their daughter and they had spoken to your great Aunt about purchasing the property in the New Year.'
'I wouldn't pay attention to that nonsense.' Robert looked more uncomfortable in his chair. He stood up, 'anybody want a top up?' Both Eric and Robbie handed their empty glasses to Robert but his failed attempt to divert the conversation had not worked.
'Wow, I didn't even realize my aunt was looking to sell.' Eric said. Robert looked perturbed but moved to the back of the room to fill their drinks.
'I'm not sure she is, I think it's more the Fox's wanting the property and trying to convince your Aunt.' Kailey said. 'I had a snoop on

Google, and from what I can gather about the Fox's they have the money to make a good offer, so watch this space.'

'Sorry Mrs Claypole, I neglected to make you a drink, can I get you anything?' Robert's made another attempt to change the direction of the conversation. He handed Eric and Robbie full glasses and waited for her response.

'Why not? I'll have a malt whisky please; will help me sleep this evening and it seems suited to this fire and the snow outside.' She smiled at Robert.

'Very wise choice' he said and turned back towards the drinks.

'I don't really come here often anymore but it'll be strange the thought of my Auntie not being at the Hotel.' Eric said.

'Why don't you come anymore?' Kailey asked.

'Just haven't come since I was younger with family, and then the years fly by and before you know it, 25 years have passed.'

'Well just in case this is the last year, let's make sure it's a good send off for Christmas!' Robbie said and raised his glass to clink it with Eric's, Eric obliged and smiled as he clinked the glasses together before taking a sip of his drink.

‘Here you go my dear.’ Robert leaned over the back of the sofa and passed a glass to Kailey.

‘Thank you’ she replied as took it and she lifted her legs onto the sofa, curling up with the drink. Robert walked back towards the large window which had its curtains pulled bar a small gap between the two adjoining sides. It was dark outside so it was difficult to see how the weather was faring. He wandered slowly over, the room was quiet as everyone reflectively looked at their drinks and the fire. Robert pulled the curtains apart and peered through the darkness.

‘Good god!’ he exulted.

‘What?’ Eric asked as Kailey swivelled round in her sofa and Robbie looked up from the fire.

‘The snow! It’s about 4 foot deep outside, its right up to the bottom of the window!’ The other guests got up from their seats and walked over to the window to examine the sight of the snow which Robert had described.

‘Whoa’ Robbie exclaimed, ‘it wasn’t like that when we got here! It must have been blizzarding outside!’

‘I don’t think I’ve ever seen the snow like that before!’ Kailey said.

'Well we'll be fine for building a snowman on Christmas day anyway' Eric smiled, 'not sure any of the staff will be heading home tomorrow though.'
'I think you might be right.' Robert said. He let the curtains fall and they closed up again, obscuring the view from the rest. Kailey leaned forward to again pull at one of the curtains so she could continue looking out across the white covered landscape. 'It snowed like this the last time I spent Christmas with my auntie Patricia coincidentally, must a Christmas tradition.' They moved back towards the seats by the fire, Kailey stayed at the window looking out as the others sat back down in their seats.
'It's lovely and cosy so I have no complaints, perfect way to spend Christmas' Robbie said.
'It definitely is festive, we just need to arrange to have a stocking of some sort each to hang from the fire, lack of a Christmas tree in here too' Eric replied. Kailey made her way back to the end of the sofa and curled back up as she sat down.
'I think Patricia is planning on putting the tree up in that corner tomorrow. The gardener has cut down one of the trees from the ground so it just needs bringing in and decorating.' Robert said. The

door was opened as Patricia and Katie walked in. Patricia had small glass cake stand in her hand, piled with mince pies, and Katie followed with a tray of sandwiches.

'Mince pies anyone?' Patricia smiled as she moved into the centre of the room.

'Perfectly timed to go with our drinks' Robert beamed, 'we just need some…' He stopped mid-sentence and his glass fell to the floor, breaking instantly, the shards of glass spreading across the floor around him.

'Oh Robert!' Patricia said.

'I'll get something to clean it up' Katie moved quickly back out the room and pulled the door closed behind her.

'Robert, really' Patricia seemed exasperated.

'I, uhm, I, sorry'

'Not a problem, we'll get this cleaned up.' Robbie and Eric had already moved to pick up the larger shards of glass.

'Oh don't defend the silly old fool; he's done nothing but drink since he arrived.' Patricia exclaimed causing Eric and Robbie to shoot a glance to each other feeling a little red in the cheeks from their own consumption of drinks.

‘Sorry, I just thought…I’ll…’ Robert stammered as he made absent minded movements towards looking for the pieces of the glass.

‘Don’t worry about it, just watch your feet’ Eric said.

‘Is there anything I can do?’ Kailey joined in, but without moving from her perch on the sofa.

‘No dear, don’t you worry about a thing’ Patricia smiled and her tone softened.

‘I think I’ll head up to my, erm, room now.’ Robert stood and carefully stood over the area of broken glass.

‘Yes I think that’ll be a good idea’ Patricia said to the rest of the room, almost rolling her eyes.

‘Goodnight’ Robert said, still with the absent minded look upon his face.

‘Good night. Was nice meeting you.’ Eric smiled looking up from scooping another shard of glass. Robert smiled and nodded and then left the room.

‘Wow, never seen alcohol hit somebody so quickly.’ Robbie said standing up.

‘Ooh don’t be fooled, he’s been at the decanters all afternoon, discreetly topping up his drink like I wouldn’t notice.’ Patricia let out a sigh, 'I will go check he's made it up to his room in a second.' Katie re-entered the room with a dust pan and brush and headed down towards where they had collected some of the shards. Robbie placed a few of the larger pieces straight into her dustpan. He got back up and sank into his seat again. 'Anyway, please help yourselves to a mince pie, there is cream and brandy butter. And Brian has prepared some warm turkey and cranberry sandwiches for you two, I can imagine you're both fairly hungry.' She smiled at Eric.

'Thank you' he and Robbie answered in unison.

'No need for thanks, but please refrain from following in Robert's footsteps this evening.' She smiled less assuredly at Robbie who happened to be taking a sip of his drink at that moment. He smiled as he lowered the glass. 'Anyway I'll leave you a little longer and then I can come join you for a mince pie myself and maybe we can have a catch up.' She smiled and turned. Katie had finished cleaning up the glass, and the two exited the room, the start of a conversation could be heard as they closed the door, and the soft mumble of voices slowly got quieter as they moved away. The fire crackled and just

Robbie, Eric, and Kailey were left by the fire, Kailey continued to stare at the flickering flames, perched on the end of the sofa.

'Never seen someone crash and burn like that before.' Robbie leaned over to Eric. Eric just nodded in agreement as he had just taken a mouthful of the sandwich which his great aunt had brought in. 'I mean, he was fine, and anyone can drop a glass, but he was mumbling all over the place afterwards.' Robbie stared at the chair where Robert had been sat and took a large bite out of his sandwich. 'Bloody hell this is good.' He said after finishing is mouthful and then taking another large bite. Eric mumbled approval amongst his own bites of the sandwich.

'As much as I would love to sit here and listen to you two eat, I might head upstairs myself.' Kailey said. She smiled at both of them as she placed two mince pies onto a plate. 'Can you say goodnight to Patricia for me if she comes back in?'

'Course. Nice to meet you, see you in the morning' Eric replied. Robbie waved a goodnight with his hand, his mouth full of sandwich. She moved past the chairs and headed out of the room. The two sat in relative silence whilst they finished their sandwiches. Eric put his plate down on the table beside him and closed his eyes, realizing how tired he was after the days walk. The room had a cosy glow which emanated from the fire which added to his desire to drift to sleep and the drinks of whisky had relaxed his mind.

'Fancy another drink?' Robbie broke the Eric's tranquillity. 'I'm having a couple of them mince pies, it's Christmas so I am going for it on the indulgence.' Eric offered Robbie his empty glass and nodded.

'I presume we're going to drink until one of us drags the other to his room anyway.'

'Sounds cracking.' Robbie said and took his glass heading back to the table with the drinks. He lifted the decanter which was now half empty, they had made more of an impact on the whisky than he thought, but they were in no danger of running short, there was about 6 other decanters behind the whisky one they had been drinking from. Robbie filled both their glasses and headed back to sit down.

'So what do you think?' he asked.

'About what?'

'The other guests?'

'Everyone seems nice.' Eric said, Robbie nodded and sat and thought to himself.

‘Not sure your aunt likes me though.’

‘I’m not sure she does either, but she’s like that with everyone and we are here now and we have food and drink, so just enjoy it.’

‘I am but how can I be comfortable with that? Especially now you agree she doesn’t like me?’ Eric smiled back at Robbie.

‘I’m just messing, she’s just strict like I said she used to be a head teacher. Comes with the territory.’

‘I guess.’ Robbie said reflectively. ‘What about the blogger?’

‘Kailey?’ Robbie nodded. ‘I think she seems nice.’

‘Withdrawn I’d say, I guess that’s social media people for you. She’d be happier tweeting us.’

‘I thought she seemed nice’ Eric said laughing.

‘And the illusive Foxs who I presume we overheard slagging off your aunt’

‘Yeah that was a little weird but I guess if they are talking about buying the place maybe my aunt drives a hard bargain.’

‘Bugger me.’ Robbie suddenly said.

‘What?’

'These mince pies man! They're amazing.' He said cleaning the remnants of crumbs from around his lap. Robbie got up and headed back towards the table of drinks, he hadn't finished his drink yet.
'You're smashing that whisky' Eric said surprised. Robbie shook his head and showed Eric his half full glass in his hand. He picked up the decanter of whisky and turned back around.
'Why take a horse to water, if you can bring water to the horse?' He said smiling, and grabbed another mince pie before placing the decanter between their seats on the floor.
'Don't think you've got that saying quite right but good thinking.' He smiled and dragged Robert's now vacated chair towards him and placed both his feet up. Just as he did so his Aunt entered the room causing Eric to quickly bring his feet back to the floor. The two of them looked up, Eric had the sudden sensation that the two of them had been mischievous children under her gaze. Obviously the idiosyncrasies of his aunt and her headmistress manner provoked these reactions naturally of him. His aunt closed the door quietly behind herself, almost like she did not want anyone to hear the door click.

‘Eric, I think something terrible has happened. I think Robert is dead.’

‘What?’ Eric looked at Robbie, who he noticed looked rather glazed in his expression; the alcohol was obviously starting to take a slight toll.

‘I have just been up to his room. He’s slumped on the desk in there.’ His aunt looked startled.

‘You sure he’s not just drunk, we saw him earlier.’ Robbie asked.

‘I’m not stupid.’ She snapped back at Robbie. ‘I presumed he was drunk but I can’t wake him and he is slumped like he’s had a heart attack or something.’

‘Ok well let’s go have a look, see if we can bring him round.’ Eric said.

‘What if you can’t?’

‘I’m sure he is just sleeping off his drink, you said yourself he had been drinking all day.’ He replied.

‘I know that.’ She said a little exasperated at the two of them, ‘but what if he is?’

‘What do you mean?’ Eric asked.

‘Well I haven’t said anything and now isn’t the time to go into it, but a couple of the guests here are interested in buying the hotel. What with them and Kailey and her review, I can’t have a dead body here over Christmas.’ She whispered as she said the word dead body.

‘Well let’s go have a look anyway; we’ll come to that bridge if we need to.’ Eric insinuated that his aunt lead the way and the three of them left the room.

CHAPTER 3 - 23RD OF DECEMBER

They reached Robert's room, which was the floor above Eric and Robbie's. The quick ascent up the two flights of stairs had left all of them rather gasping for air. The stairs alone were enough for a heart attack, Robbie thought to himself as he tried to steady his breath. Patricia pushed the door open, and they were immediately confronted with Robert's frame hunched over a writing desk in front of a large mirror on the wall. They walked in unison towards

Robert's body, Eric noticed how much of a mess the room was but Robert looked fairly peaceful in his chair.

'Robert' Eric said softly, almost liked his was coaxing the man to awaken. 'Robert can you hear me?' He softly pushed the large man's shoulder, he moved as he pushed him but Eric received no response.

'Robert?'

'Oy! Robert!' Robbie quickly shouted, thumping the man on the back and making both Eric and Patricia jump.

'What the hell you doing?' Eric attempted to raise his voice whilst maintaining a whispered voice.

'Why you whispering? I thought we were waking him up?' Robbie replied, bending over to see if he could see any reaction from the slumped man's face.

'Well? What do you think?' Patricia asked.

'Well he's definitely a heavy sleeper.' Eric said scratching his head. 'I'm not a doctor.'

'Try his pulse' Robbie suggested.

'What?'

'Try his pulse, and then we'll know if he's dead or not.' Robbie nodded at the body. Eric gave Robert another shove and then proceeded to pull at the man's arm which was limp at his side. He pulled up the sleeve on his arm. His body is still warm Eric thought to himself but they'd not seen any reactions from Robert to suggest he was in a drunken stupor.

'He feels a bit clammy?' Eric wasn't sure if this was a sign of life or mortality but both Robbie and Patricia stared blankly back at him. He found Roberts wrist with his two fingers and pressed hard. Robert was overweight and Eric didn't know if that would make finding a pulse harder or not, but he kept holding.

'Well?' Robbie said. Eric shrugged and shook his head. Patricia took a step back from the three of them and let out a long sigh.

'I'm not a doctor, I don't really know what I am doing.' He adjusted his fingers to try and feel around for any sign of life. Robbie leaned forward and pulled the paper from underneath Robert's resting forehead. 'I don't know if I am holding my fingers in the right place? Robbie, you have a go'. Robbie ignored Eric's suggestion and had his finger pressed to his lips in concentration.

'Hmm' he said after a few moments.

'What? Come have a go at this pulse.' Eric said. Letting go of Robert's wrist which slumped back down to the side of his chair.

‘Not sure that’s necessary.’ Robbie handed the sheet of paper over to Eric. Patricia leaned forward.

‘What is it?’ she asked. Eric scanned his eyes across the document before reading aloud.

‘Dear Patricia, it has come to my attention that neither of us is safe in this hotel. I realize this probably seems like a joke but I have gone to my room to pack and I suggest you do the same. I implore you to listen to me and not act in your usual stubborn manner. I worry that if you do not heed my warning that you will be murdered by the end of tonight. Someone from our past-’ Eric looked up.

‘Someone from our past? Someone from our past what?’ Patricia asked nervously.

‘It just ends like that.’ Eric said handing her the letter.

‘Maybe he didn’t get time to finish it?’ Robbie suggested.

‘What do you mean? Eric asked. Robbie replied with a gesture suggesting a hangman’s noose. ‘Don’t be ridiculous, you think he’s been murdered?’

‘Course I do, have you not seen the letter? He happens to say he’s in danger and then we find him slumped on his desk?’ Robbie replied.

‘Well why didn’t the murderer take the letter? And how’s he killed him? He looks fairly tranquil to me.’ Eric felt a little more assured by his own words. Robert certainly didn’t look like someone who had been attacked in anyway and looked rather at peace lay on his desk. Robbie seemed stuck in thought before replying.

‘Poison. The murderer must have poisoned him. Hence why the murderer hasn’t taken the letter because they weren’t in the room with Robert, and it’s also the reason Robert calmly sat down to write a letter before he…, you know’ Eric started blankly at Robbie. Patricia seemed to be examining the letter and seemed to be in either complete control or consumed by shock. ‘I mean, we all saw how he was drinking, would be simple enough to put something in his drink?’ Robbie carried on. Eric had no real reply to give and the letter certainly suggested that Robert felt he was in some sort of danger.

‘Oh god.’ Patricia said and steadied herself against the desk with her hand, seeming as if she was about to faint. Eric quickly grabbed her arm and steadied her.

‘Why don’t you have a seat Auntie?’ and he edged her towards the end of the bed before sitting her down. Eric turned and looked at

Robbie and gestured a look of uncertainty of how to proceed, Robbie shrugged his shoulders in reply. Eric didn't know what to say to alleviate the situation, his mind was running with the potential discovery that there was a murderer in the hotel and they had witnessed a murder. 'Would you like a drink or anything Auntie?' Eric asked but his great aunt seemed a little despondent.

'I wouldn't' Robbie said. Eric glared at Robbie, 'what, I mean if Robert was poisoned, and with the warning etc...' Eric intensified his glare at Robbie who had been oblivious to the nature of Eric's first glare which had been intended to shut him up. Robbie then cottoned on 'Oh right, yeah, it'll be fine, I'll get a glass of water from the bathroom.' He turned quickly and entered the small bathroom which was part of the room's interior.

'Do you think it's true?' Patricia meekly said with her head low.

'What's that auntie?' Eric asked in a soothing tone.

'The warning? Do you think I am unsafe here?'

'I think we'll be fine once we notify the police, nothing for you to worry about.' Eric answered just as Robbie came back into the room with a glass of water. He attempted to silently mouth *I've washed it* but it was clear what he had said, Patricia made no reaction but took the glass from Eric and took a sip.

'What now?' Robbie asked.

'Well we can give the police a call, and we can just sit here until they sort it all out.'

'We can't' Patricia said as she looked up at the pair.

'We can't what auntie?'

'There is no way of calling the police. Or any emergency service.'

'What do you mean?' Eric asked.

'There is no mobile reception at the hotel, it's one of the perks we offer in our packages for complete relaxation.'

'Well what about the phones and internet etc.? We can just use either of them.'

'They have both been down since this morning. I don't know if it was the snow or what but I haven't been able to get through to anyone to fix it. Our handyman George hasn't answered any of the internal calls but he has probably gone home for the holidays now anyway.' Eric and Robbie exchanged glances at this piece of information. 'Do you really think we can't get to your car?' she implored rather timidly. The strong willed manner of Patricia had quickly dissipated she had begun to realise the situation they were in.

'It's only got worse since we managed to fight through' Eric said shaking his head.

'We could just stay in here until the morning and it may have melted a little anyway?' Robbie suggested. 'I'll go get some drinks and food?' he said enthusiastically.

'We can't spend the night in here with a dead body.' Eric said a little exasperated with Robbie.

'Ah so he is dead?' Robbie looked at Eric.

'Course he's dead, what are you talking about?'

'Well just earlier you didn't seem to agree when I suggested he was dead. I just wanted confirmation.' Robbie smiled to himself.

'Will you two shut up.' Patricia said. 'I am not staying in here with a body all night; one of you or both of you can escort me to my room.' She began to stand, putting out her arm for Eric to support her. As she stood, there was a faint knock at the door of the room. They all stopped moving, Eric and Robbie looked at each other again. Patricia sat unsteadily back down on the edge of the bed. They waited but there was no further knock at the door.

'Shall I open the door?' Eric enquired looking at the two in turn.

'No, I don't want the other guests finding out about this.' Patricia said after a moment.

'Auntie, they are going to find out eventually, the police will want to know about all this, you can't hide it.'

'Ok but there is no point saying anything as yet, we will only scare everybody this evening, especially as we have no way of contacting the police.'

'I've just had a thought.' Robbie interjected ignoring the conversation of the other two. 'If this was a murder, and Robert was poisoned-' He looked back at Robert's slumped body, 'the murderer wouldn't necessarily know if Robert was dead yet or not.'

'So? What are you saying?' Eric asked.

'Well couldn't the mysterious knock at the door been made by our murderer? Seeing if Robert was still alive?' Neither Eric or Patricia answered nor did they dismiss Robbie's suggestion. Before either of them could reply, there was another knock at the door making them all startle. Eric considered walking to the door and opening to see who was so desperate to see Robert but he changed his mind after thinking over what Robbie had said. *Why would anybody be knocking at Robert's door at this time?* It was only really Patricia who had any tie to Robert and she was currently sat slumped on the edge of the now deceased Robert's bed. There was then another knock at the door.

'Hello? Mr Wilson, are you ok?' the voice said from behind the door.

'It's Katie.' Said Patricia looking up at Eric and Robbie.

'Should we let her in?' Robbie asked.

Before Eric could answer, the door was opened and in walked Katie, turning and closing the door behind herself. She turned and jumped as she saw the three of them in the room.

'What are you doing in here? Didn't you hear me knock-' she broke off as she looked past Robbie and at Robert's frame craned forward over his desk '- what's going on?'

'Why are you here?' Robbie asked inquisitively. Katie looked slightly taken aback by the question, then she looked at the other two and noticed they were both looking directly at her in the same way as Robbie.

'I-I came to check on Robert after his turn downstairs. I thought he may have been embarrassed and was going to offer him a drink. I just saw Mrs Fox outside the room, she left when she saw me and I thought maybe there was a problem.' She looked at Robert again, 'why are you all here? And what's going on with Mr Wilson?'

'You saw Mrs Fox outside?' Eric asked.

'Yes, just before I came in, what on earth is going on here?'

Eric looked at Robbie and then back at Katie. 'We think somebody may have murdered Robert.' He stared at Katie to analyse her reaction. She quickly clasped a hand to her mouth.

'What do you mean murdered? How do you know? Oh my god - is he dead?' She signalled towards the body slumped on the desk. Eric nodded. 'Well we need to call the police or something, why are you all in here?' She looked at the three of them.

'We think Patricia may be in danger, she may have even been the target.' Eric replied.

'Why do you think that? Is this some kind of stupid joke?' Her voice took a harsher tone as she looked at Eric and Robbie.

'It's not a joke Katie.' Patricia said as she stood up from the bed.

'Would you mind taking me back to mind room Katie?' Patricia asked. Eric noticed how much frailer she looked all of a sudden; the shock of Robert had removed the strong exterior and left a much older looking woman before him.

'Course I will.' Katie moved forward and steadied Patricia and moved her forward past Eric and Robbie.

'We better come along too Auntie.' Eric said and nodded at Robbie.

'No, there is no need. Anyone I feel a lot safer with Katie looking after me than you two.' Her sharpness seemed to recover and straight away the colour seemed to flood back into her cheeks. 'Good night to both of you.' She turned and moved towards the door. Katie looked at them both, looked past them at Robert, and then turned and followed Patricia out the room.

'Do you think she'll be ok? Should we go with them?' Robbie asked.

'She said not, but we could always camp it out tonight outside her room?'

'Why don't we stay in here? We're just a few doors down and we can enjoy a bed.'

'Not with a dead body.' Eric replied rather disgustedly. 'Anyway we can keep watch on the corridor if we stay up out there.'

'All night?' Robbie said surprisingly.

'I guess, we can always take shifts maybe?'

‘Right, fine. But I’m off downstairs to get some provisions if we’re having a stake out.’ Eric nodded at this suggestion by Robbie who had already started for the door.

‘Hey, I’ve just thought of something.’ Eric said.

‘Go on’. Robbie said as he opened the door.

‘If there hasn’t been any phone service since yesterday, how did Katie get through to her boyfriend?’

‘Hmm, I hadn’t thought of that. She’s either telling the truth and we can use her phone to call the police or she’s lied to us.’ They closed the door behind them, pushing the handle again to make sure it had locked. ‘Plus she has a key to this room.’

‘And maybe all the other rooms too.’ Eric finished Robbie’s thought process. ‘Come on, let’s get our stuff and head back up here quick.’

Eric sat slumped against the hotel corridor wall. His aunt’s room door was to his left and opposite him Robbie sat in an identical slumped position against the adjacent wall. They had brought themselves a pillow each taken from Eric’s room, and Robbie had gone downstairs to grab a bottle of port and some mince pies. Eric had lambasted him for leaving the sandwiches which he pointed out would have provided a more nutritious meal to keep them both going but Robbie had argued that the mince pies would complement the Port better. Robbie had also been quick to point out that he had brought an unopened bottle in case the poison was anywhere else to be found.

'What time is it?' Eric asked wearily.

'Quarter past two.' Robbie replied looking down at his watch before having another sip from his small port glass. Eric looked at him, unbelieving that Robbie had the foresight to bring port glasses but nothing substantial to eat. 'It's Christmas Eve!' he said with a smile, 'I'd sort have forgotten.'

'My weirdest Christmas Eve so far.' Eric said.

'So who do you reckon is after your aunt?'

'We don't even know anyone is after her. The note might have been left there after he died just to scare my aunt.' This thought had not come to Eric previously but now he had said it aloud, it seemed quite conceivable. 'Actually that would explain why Mrs Fox was outside the room, maybe she had something to do with, obviously the Fox's want to buy the place and maybe they want to scare my aunt off?'

‘That’s not a bad idea actually.’ Robbie seemed impressed with Eric’s suggestion. ‘But then again, they were either hoping Robert would die so this plan could come off, or they killed him which still makes them murderers, and if they are murderers then logically they could still come for your aunt.’ This thought quickly put paid to Eric’s suggestion. However if they had somehow come across the body of Robert before his aunt, they could have acted quickly to make the natural death look more suspicious than it actually was. Eric leaned his head back against the hotel wall with a thud.

‘Do you think we should tell everybody else tomorrow?’

‘I don’t know, what if one of them is the murderer?’ Robbie said.

‘Unless somebody has braved the snow, or been hidden somewhere in the hotel, the likelihood is one of the guests is the murderer.’

‘We haven’t even met all of them yet.’

‘I reckon it was that robotic like receptionist. What was his name?’

‘I can’t remember, but he was a little off. Then again, I can’t see why he would be someone from their past.’

‘I suppose not. Who would be from your aunt’s past who knew Robert as well? A family member? As Robert pointed out, you don’t know them all.’

'Yes but my aunt would have surely recognized any family members straight away.' Eric said, 'maybe it was someone from the school she worked at?'

'Yes but why would they have gone for Robert?' Robbie asked, taking a bite out of another mince pie.

'Not sure. Hang on actually, Robert was a student at my aunt's school when she was headmistress.'

'Ah, so someone from their past could easily be someone from the school. But wouldn't they be ancient too? The Fox's aren't old enough, and neither is anybody else we have met.'

'That's true, and he did say someone from the past.'

'Anyway what on earth would have happened at the school for all these years to have passed before somebody sought vengeance? I mean how bad was your aunt?'

Eric stared at Robbie not saying anything. 'Wow, that bad eh?'

'She was old school, she didn't hit anyone but she was strict, slamming tables etc. I remember my mum saying ex-students used to regularly vandalize her home and stuff.'

'Hmm, well if one of the Fox's was an ex pupil, wouldn't she recognize them?'

'I haven't a clue to be honest.' Eric replied. 'But we have no way of knowing if it has anything to do with the school.'

'I think there is something fishy about Katie.' Robbie said. Eric looked at him before gesturing for him to continue. 'Well, it was when she walked in the room that Robert suddenly went all weird and headed to his room. Plus she was the one who knocked on the door and let herself in to Robert's room.'

'That's true.'

'Plus! She lied to us about making a phone call for some reason. I say we keep an eye on her.'

'My aunt seems to trust her.' Eric said.

'Who else do we have? The weird reception guy; Kailey the subdued blogger who doesn't seem that happy to be spending Christmas here.'

'Hardly grounds for murder though is it?' Eric said.

'Yeah but she might just be a loony, but I guess that doesn't explain Robert's letter. Then we have the Fox family, they could all be in cahoots, and money is a great motivator for murder. Who else is there?'

‘Well there is a gardener apparently who we haven’t met, and the same with the renowned chef.’ Eric said. ‘Surely he would have used a classic knife being a chef and all.’

‘Hey this is quite exciting, an old fashioned whodunit in a hotel set at Christmas.’ Robbie said.

‘You could say that I guess. But I still think we should try making it out of here tomorrow and speaking to the police.’ Eric yawned as he finished his sentence. ‘Shall we try get some sleep? Set your alarm and wake me up in like an hour?’

‘Fine by me, but don’t expect any Port to be left.’ He lifted the bottle and unscrewed the cork like lid which gave a squeak and proceeded to pour himself another small glass. Eric plumped up his pillow on the floor and lay down, the hard floor of the corridor was far from the most comfortable of beds but he was tired enough that he didn’t really care. They had a long day tomorrow if they were going to try and make it to the village and then from there to somewhere they could contact the police or at least get a phone signal. His body still felt tired from the long trek to the hotel, and he felt apprehensive about having to make the return journey but he could quickly feel the exertion of the day weighing heavy on his mind as he quickly drifted to sleep.

CHAPTER 4 – 24TH OF DECEMBER

'Fine pair of bodyguards you two are.' Katie's voice woke Eric up from his slumber. The corridor was now lit with a natural light coming through the window at the end of the corridor. Eric's head felt a little woozy from the port last night but he blinked a few times and looked up at Katie who was stood above him with her hands on her hips. 'Were you ready to jump into action?' She smiled as Eric pushed himself up from the floor.

‘What time is it?’ He looked across at the sleeping Robbie who was stirring but hadn’t opened his eyes yet.’

‘Just after 9. I trust you enjoyed your first night in the hotel?’ Katie was smiling to herself enjoying the state of the two men sleeping in the corridor.

‘What happened?’ Eric addressed Robbie who was now starting to wake up too.

‘I must have drifted off.’ Robbie said sleepily.

‘You don’t say?’ Eric replied. He looked back up towards Katie ‘We best check on my aunt.’

‘You idiots, she has been downstairs since 7. She is always up early.’ Eric got himself up and stretched out his body.

‘Is she ok?’

‘No, she was attacked in the night.’ Katie replied sarcastically but smiling. ‘Anyway I came to let you two sleeping beauties know that breakfast is downstairs if you’re hungry.’

‘Great! I’m starving’ Robbie said as he sat up from his pillow.

‘I’ll go get cleaned up and then come downstairs.’ Eric said. ‘Thank you for waking us up.’

'No problem at all. I have spoken to Patricia this morning about Robert. She is going to tell the other guests, but I think any chance of us walking down to the village has gone. It has started snowing again this morning and the snow drifts are fairly high.'

'Well we can see how bad it is after breakfast.' Eric replied.

'Suit yourself. See you downstairs.' Katie said and she turned away and headed back towards the door leading to the stairs. Eric turned back to Robbie.

'You idiot, fat lot of use we were last night.'

'Yeah sorry about that, all that Port and Mince Pies must have had more of an effect that I thought.' Robbie jumped up to his feet.

'Right, let's go get some breakfast.'

'Morning all.' Robbie said as he and Eric walked through the door to the room where the other guests were eating breakfast. A chorus of murmured replies greeted them both. The room's large windows shone through the morning sunlight, and it was obvious how much snow had fallen. Robbie and Eric sat down at a table by themselves but it appeared that Patricia had told the rest of the guests what had occurred in the night as there appeared to be a melancholic feel around the room. Either that or the guests were that way inclined thought Eric to himself. Kailey was sat with the Fox family, which Eric realised also included a young daughter of about fourteen who resembled her mother strongly. Both she and Kailey were scrutinising their phones in their hands, whilst Mr and Mrs Fox were sat eating their breakfast in silence at the same table. Katie came through a door with a tray laden with tea cups and both a cafetiere and teapot and headed over to Robbie and Eric's table.

'Morning you two, tea? Coffee?' She asked as she placed the tray down on their table.

'Tea for me please' Said Robbie.

'Yes, tea for me too please.' Replied Eric as Katie proceeded to pour them both a tea from the teapot.

'Either of you two vegetarians?' Katie asked. They both shook their heads, 'you happy with full English this morning then?'

'Definitely' Robbie replied enthusiastically.

'Yes that would be lovely, thank you'. Eric said. 'Is my Aunt around?'

'She is talking to Brian at the moment, she'll probably be out shortly.' Katie replied, 'I think she is having the tough job of explaining to Brian that he will most likely be spending Christmas at the hotel too.'

'You don't seem too downbeat?' Eric said. Katie certainly did seem pleasantly joyful this morning, her radiance was a stark contrast to the gloom of the guests say at the other table.

'I don't mind really, Patricia said we can have the place to ourselves like guests and she is still going to pay us in full if we help out a little, and she said we can have the time off after Christmas. She has been very kind about it all.' Katie smiled.

'Sounds fair, aren't you going to miss family and boyfriend over Christmas?' Robbie asked inquisitively.

'I can see them after Christmas, I mean it is only one day, I can delay Christmas this year. And to be honest, what a wonderful place to spend Christmas, I was jealous of you all sat having a drink by the fire last night, so hopefully I can join you this evening.'

'That would be lovely' Eric smiled back.

'Even with the… what happened last night?' Robbie asked.

'We'll just have to make the best of it, and all of us stick together the best we can until the snow clears or the phones are repaired.' She said it under her breath somewhat which made Eric think that maybe the guests were not yet aware of what had happened last night.

'Have the rest of the staff taken the news as well as you?' Eric changed the subject in case the other table were unaware and started to listen in. The silence from the table suggested they were all listening in to the conversation at their table.

'Maybe not as well as me.' Katie paused, as she considered how much to elaborate. 'We think George, who works on the grounds and is our general handyman must have left before the snow got bad as we haven't heard from him. Patricia is telling Brian now, but I can't imagine he will take it too well. Joe took it very badly.'

'Really? Can't see him showing all that much emotion.' Robbie said, looking at them both. Katie smiled in agreement.

'Apparently he was going to spend Christmas and New Years in sunnier climbs with his family. Looks like he'll miss his flight and he doesn't know if his insurance will cover it. Obviously he can't ring and check because of the phones.'

'Ouch' Robbie replied.

'Yeah, he wasn't best pleased. Anyway, I'll go see if your food is ready to bring out.' She turned quickly after picking up the tray from

the table and headed back through the door she had come from. Before the door had finished swinging, Patricia came through the door into the breakfast room and headed towards Eric and Robbie smiling as she did. She seemed to have rejuvenated overnight and seemed fuller of energy and her usual proud posture had returned. Before she reached the table, Mr Fox turned to get her attention.
'Ermm Mrs Bradshaw, have we any further news on reaching the outside world? Or any sign we will be able to have the internet and phone lines repaired?'
'I'm afraid not Mr Fox. I will inform you as soon as anything is repaired, my first priority is to contact the ambulance and the police, and then ensure you are all -'
'The police? Why do they need contacting for a heart attack?' Mrs Fox now joined in the conversation, as Kailey looked up, also seeking a response to the question. *Heart attack? So that is how she informed the guests* Eric thought to himself, no wonder they had been rather subdued, surely a murder would have caused more discussion at the breakfast table.
'It's just procedure and I was hoping that they would have more within their power to ensure we were reached as soon as possible.

Obviously, a dead body isn't the highest priority for ambulances over Christmas.' This response from Patricia appeared to appease Mrs Fox who turned back to her lukewarm cup of tea which she had been cradling in her hands. 'If I hear anything in the meantime, I will let you all know. Let's just make the best of Christmas Eve together.' Patricia then turned back to Eric and Robbie, 'I have a little favour to ask of the two of you.' Before she could finish, the chair of the Fox family daughter shot back and she stood up, looking down at her parents with an adolescent fury.

'This is horrible! I didn't want to come here but you dragged me along and away from my friends! At Christmas too! And now I have no way of speaking to any of them with no internet! Thank you for making me feel so lonely at Christmas! I hate this place! It's like a prison!' She turned and stormed out the breakfast room.

'Quite.' Patricia turned back from the outburst to look at Eric and Robbie. Eric could see the sheepish awkward smile emanating from the face of Mrs Fox who had obviously been embarrassed by the outburst. Mr Fox remained aloof and took a sip of his coffee.

'I was wondering if you two would be able to go down to our maintenance shed after you've both had some breakfast. I realise it's still snowing but it's only around a mile roundtrip so it's not like the journey you made up to the hotel.'

'I know Auntie, but the snow is even worse now.' Eric protested a little, Robbie looked from Eric to Patricia and gave a hurried nod in agreement.

'I realise that but you might be able to find out why the internet and phones are down, you might even possibly get a phone signal down there if you take your mobiles.' She leaned in a little closer and followed up with a whisper, 'I'm also slightly concerned that I haven't heard from our handyman George for a few days. He has probably gone home for Christmas but I don't want to find another dead body in the hotel grounds.' She stood back up straight again, 'I won't ask another thing of you both and there'll be warm festive food waiting for you when you get back, and I'll share my finest brandy with you too' she aimed the brandy comment at Robbie smiling, oblivious to the obvious bribery from Patricia.

'Fine.' Eric let out a loud sigh, 'we'll finish our breakfast and then go check it out.'

'Wonderful' Patricia smiled at both and clasped her hands together.

‘I don’t mean to pry -’ Kailey from the other table has leaned forward, ‘but would there be any chance of me joining you? I wouldn’t mind some fresh air and I’d love to see if I can get a signal for my phone.’ She looked inquisitively at all three in turn. Patricia looked rather skittish at the proposal.

‘The weather is awfully bad my dear, maybe we should see if they can ascertain whether there is a signal first?’ Patricia smiled at Kailey.

‘I don’t mind, I’ve been in worse snow that outside before’ she looked at Eric and Robbie, ‘let me know when you’re setting off and I’ll join you both.’ She beamed a smile as she stood up from the table. ‘That is of course if you don’t mind the company?’

‘Uh no, of course not.’ Eric said, and Robbie shook his head.

‘Great!’ she turned and looked at Patricia, ‘Thank you for breakfast.’ She then moved away from the table and left the room.

‘Well I didn’t really want that to happen but she seemed fairly insistent.’ Patricia remarked, ‘if you do find anything untoward, can you try and ensure she isn’t recording it all for her internet activities, that’s the last thing I need right now.’ She looked sternly at the two of them, her usual stricter tone returning.

Eric and Robbie finished their breakfast, and by that time they were the only two left, as the Fox's had departed not long after their food had arrived. After sitting in a content mood following breakfast, basking in the tranquillity of the breakfast room, they had decided to get the trip down to the maintenance shed out the way so they could enjoy the rest of the day. Despite what had happened the night before, relative normality had returned to the hotel, and Patricia had decided to decorate the Christmas tree, which Eric and Robbie would help bring in after their trip. Apparently Joe was planned to help Patricia and Katie but had gone on strike since learning that he would not be leaving the hotel. He had ventured outside to attempt the walk to the road but had returned 5 minutes later in even more of a foul mood. Eric and Robbie couldn't believe that the slightly robotic Joe would demonstrate such emotions but they had not seen him all day. After changing and putting on their warmer clothes they headed back downstairs, Robbie had let Kailey know they were getting ready and expected to meet her downstairs. Walking through the doors into the reception area, Kailey, Joe, Patricia, and Katie were all in the reception, as was a rather wet looking large Christmas tree on its side.

‘I thought you wanted us to help you with that when we got back?’ Eric asked as the two got closer to the rest of the group.

‘We thought we would get it up and decorated for when you got back. Will take everyone’s mind off Robert and the lack of internet.’ Katie smiled back, she had obviously been outside as her clothes were damp up to her waist.

‘And Joe, kindly agreed to help.’ Patricia said smiling at Joe. He returned a blank expression in her direction.

‘May as well as that my plans for Christmas have been ruined.’ He said sarcastically smiling at Robbie and Eric.

‘Ok.’ Robbie rolled his eyes, and looked to Kailey, ‘you ready to join us then?’

‘Sure am. Let’s get going.’ Robbie stuck out an arm insinuiating that she lead the way. Robbie and then Eric followed Kailey as she went out the front door. The sun was shining brightly and almost blinded the three of them as they headed outside, the sun reflecting of the blanket of snow covering the ground. They could see where Joe and Katie had dragged the Christmas tree, and the flattened path of the tree accentuated how deep the rest of the snow was, it was almost four foot in areas around the hotel.

‘This isn’t going to be that easy.’ Eric said.

‘Do we know where we are going?’ Kailey asked, the steam from her breath was crisp against the cold air.

‘Apparently we will be able to see it once we get to that mound.’ Eric pointed away from the hotel across an unspoiled vast sea of snow. Robbie and Kailey, both put a hand above their eyes to block the sun as they looked towards where Eric was pointing. ‘Would only take ten or fifteen minutes if the weather was ok, might take us double that with the snow?’

‘Well, we best get going!’ Robbie said and took the first few steps into the deep snow with enthusiasm, but he soon changed to dragging his legs to wade through the snow. The other two followed him, their path made easier by the flattened snow Robbie left behind.

‘We can swap round when you’re tired.’ Kailey shouted forward to Robbie.

‘Fancy changing now then?’ he turned smiling with already reddened cheeks from the exhaustion. They trudged on through the snow, after a while Robbie stopped, turning around panting.

‘Anyone fancying switching for a bit?’ He said between breaths.

‘Go on, I’ll have a go for a bit. At least it’ll be quicker on the way back.’ Eric turned and looked where they had come, they could see the solitary flattened line trailing through the snow.

‘I’ve never seen anything like it before.’ Kailey said, ‘I mean we rarely get a white Christmas, let alone snow like this.’

‘Bingo!’ Robbie said smiling, ‘I just remembered I put a bet on there being a White Christmas this year.’ He stuck a gloved thumb up the air to the other two, as he moved past Eric, who replaced him stood at the front of the unfettered snow.

‘I thought it was only a white Christmas if it was actually snowing on Christmas day?’ Kailey said.

‘She’s right, snow on the ground doesn’t count, you need snow in the air.’

‘Well that’s bound to happen, this morning is the first time it has stopped snowing for about 4 days.’ Robbie replied.

‘Doesn’t mean it will tomorrow.’ Eric smiled, and he trudged into the snow, taking the lead in clearing a footpath for the other two. Robbie turned to Kailey and mimicked Eric’s comment silently. Eric continued ‘I don’t think Joe would have got very far on his flight even if he had got away this morning, I can't imagine flights are taking off from here.'

'That's exactly what I said to him this morning, but he bit my head off.' Kailey said.

'At you?' Robbie asked.

'Yeah, he was really wound up about missing his flights, and having to be at the hotel over Christmas. Katie told me he stormed in after attempting to get to the road on foot. I mentioned that his flight may have been cancelled anyway because of the snow so he might just get a refund. And then he had a pop at me, saying that it was ok for people like me spending Christmas alone in a hotel as I have no friends who weren't online.'

'Seems kinda harsh.' Eric said.

'I know, and then he stormed off. But he seemed fine when he came to help with the tree but he still seems a bit prickly like anything could set him off again.' Kailey continued.

'Where was he going anyway?' Robbie asked.

'Not sure, he didn't say. Well he didn't tell me anyway. Katie apologised for him after though; she said that he has family issues and Christmas is quite hard for him.'

'Fair enough, but still doesn't justify having a go at you.' Robbie said.

'Apparently, his mum is in some kind of care institute and his dad committed suicide when he was younger. I think Katie told me to try and explain why he's a bit, you know - '

'Cooky' Robbie said and Kailey nodded. They continued walking through the snow, most of the time they walked in silence as the exertion of wading through the snow left them all panting a little. Kailey took a go at the front before Robbie took over and lead them the last of the way towards the maintenance shed.

'I don't think there is anybody here, the snow looks fairly untouched.' Eric said. 'Might have been a wasted journey I am afraid.'

'Not wasted, your aunt promised us a festive treat when we get back, so it's worth it to me.' Robbie walked up the wooden steps to the shed.

'So this is where he lives?' Kailey asked.

'No, he lives somewhere down in the village, but he works from here apparently.' Eric glanced around the side of the hut but no foot prints suggested that anyone had been here for a few days. 'He must have just gone home for Christmas, my aunt did say that he may have just gone home.'

'She is probably just a little worried after what happened last night.' Kailey said. Robbie and Eric looked at each other. 'I mean having to stumble across a family member dead must have been awful for her.'

'Yeah.' Robbie said. He said so as he simultaneously as he checked the door, which opened when he gave the handle a push.

'It's open?' Eric said and came up behind Robbie quickly.

'No sign of any handyman in here but somebody has definitely done a number on the place.' Robbie said. Eric pushed his head past what Robbie was looking at. The maintenance hut inside had been completely vandalised. It looked like a stereotypically depicted vandalism, chairs were upturned, and electric cables were sprouting from different areas on the control desk.

'Wow, they had some serious electronic gear down here.' Robbie said, as he stepped inside, 'but they have just trashed it all, I mean why didn't they just rob the place?'

'Woah' Kailey said as she followed the two inside. 'You think this is why the internet and phones aren't working?'

‘Yeah could be I guess.’ Eric replied, pushing broken parts of the control table with his foot on the floor. ‘I wouldn’t have a clue how to repair any of this stuff anyway.’

‘Your aunt is not going to be happy.’ Robbie said, ‘did you think this was done by the same person who - ’ Robbie looked at Kailey and stopped mid-sentence. It was already too late as Kailey had seen him abruptly stop as he caught her eye.

‘Same person who what?’ Kailey looked at Robbie and then Eric. ‘What do you mean?’

‘Somebody let my tyres down in the village on our way here, but I think these are just coincidences.’ Eric said looking at Kailey.

Robbie nodded quickly. Kailey stared back at Eric but didn’t say anything in reply. She held his gaze for a while, and Eric was on the verge of adding to his lie before she smiled.

‘Well we may as well get back to the hotel anyway. No sign of the handyman, and I don’t think we can manage to fix anything down here.’ She said and she turned and pushed her way back outside. Eric looked at Robbie as he headed towards the down and gave him a backhanded slap with his hand on his arm.

‘What? You covered it’ he said shrugging before following Eric out the door. He pushed the door closed, and they followed Kailey back through the path of flattened snow.

After reaching the hotel a little later, the atmosphere inside seemed much brightened from the rather glum breakfast. Even Joe was smiling with Katie when they got back to the hotel. Between Joe, Katie, and Patricia, they had managed to stand the large Christmas tree into a stand and placed it inside the main room where they had all sat the night before. Whilst the fire was not yet lit, the room took on an instant festive feel as the smell of pine needles had filled the room. Kailey had headed straight up to her room after they arrived back at the hotel and told both Eric and Robbie that she wanted to get changed. Robbie and Eric had simple taken off their boots and hung their coats by the door. Patricia had come through the reception just as they were hanging their coats and told them that she had decided to allow the guests to decorate the tree in order to lift everyone’s spirits. Robbie had giddily agreed and headed straight in the direction of the room and Eric followed after him.

‘Wow, can you smell that?’ Robbie said after a large inhale of air, ‘That is Christmas my friend.’

‘Do you think we should wait for the others?’

‘Your aunt said to head straight in. Kailey will be down in a bit and I don’t reckon the gloomy Fox family will be interested.’

‘Yeah but maybe people want to come join the festivities?’ Eric asked.

‘Look, I am not having my Christmas ruined because of some scrooges who happen to be staying here too. Murder aside, I plan on enjoying the rest of my time here.’ Robbie picked a lid off a box which had been placed by the tree. ‘Lights on first?’

‘Go on then.’ Eric headed over as Robbie began pulling the lights out of the box, the tangled mess fell to the floor as he held it up to untangle the different lights.

‘That snow wasn’t too bad on the way to that shed today; you reckon we could make the road?’ Robbie asked.

‘I think it would be harder, I mean the walk up to the hotel was harder than that walk today and that was a few days ago.’

‘That’s true.’

‘Anyway even if we did finally get down to the road, what would we do? The road was already covered then so it would probably be worse now. It wasn't like it was a main road so I can't imagine them clearing it on Christmas Eve.'

'But what about the hotel?' Robbie asked. 'Surely, they will have thought that they need access on the road to the hotel?'

'Yeah but they may have tried calling here, found the lines dead and assumed that the place was closed.'

'Can't imagine them even being that thorough, looks like we are well and truly snowed in.' Robbie said. The two of them pulled apart the length of the lights until they were completely untangled. Eric collected one end as he disappeared around the back of the tree.

'There's a plug back here so we can use this, so start winding it around.' Robbie pulled the lights, intertwining them between the lower branches of the tree before passing the length of lights to Eric to continue pulling the lights around.

'I've just had a thought.' Robbie said, as he went to receive the length of lights from Eric and began to pull them around the tree again but on a higher level of the branches.

'Go on.' Eric replied from behind the tree.

‘Well obviously we are stuck here. But what if our murderer wanted to do the crime and then escape himself? I mean the murderer is trapped here too.’

‘Yeah well I can’t imagine anyone from outside the hotel making it here, committing the murder, and then going again without anyone noticing.’ Eric said.

‘I know, exactly. So that means the murderer’s plans have probably been thwarted too as he is -’

‘or she is’ Eric added, as he passed the lights back around to Robbie.

‘yeah or she, is stuck in the hotel too.’

‘And? Isn’t that an obvious statement? We’re all stuck here.’ Eric said.

‘Yes but if you wanted to get away with murder, escaping before anyone realised would be a good port of call. Once we all know about the murder, then the murderer will know the police are going to be here at some point and no one will be able to leave.’

‘Right? And?’

‘Well, what if the murderer thinks their next best option is to kill everybody here and then escape before anyone decides to check out the hotel which has been closed for Christmas?’

‘What if they’re not that brutal?’

‘Well if they want to get away with it, it would be their only real option.’ Robbie replied.

‘So you’re saying we should make sure this is kept a secret?’

‘Well yeah, so far everyone believes it was a heart attack, which probably suits the killer fine.’

‘What if the killer is Katie? She knows.’ Eric said.

‘Yeah and so does your Aunt.’

‘What? Is she on your suspect list?’

‘Of course, she found the body, you’d be on there too but I’m giving you the benefit of the doubt.’

‘Thanks.’ Eric replied dryly.

‘If the killer discovers that everyone knows that there was a murder and is trapped here for the next few days, he might decide to just bump the rest of us off.’

‘What a lovely thought.’ Eric said.

‘Precisely.’ Robbie rested the cable on the branches of the tree, ‘I’m getting a drink.’

‘What? After that spiel about a killing spree?’

‘Exactly, I want to go out happy if it does happen, and anyway, it’s after 12 now so drinking is perfectly allowed.’ Robbie had already reached the drinks table. After inspecting the glass thoroughly, he decided it was safe. ‘You not wanting one?’

‘Ah what the hell, go on.’ Robbie poured them both a drink, before carrying the bottle and the two glasses back over to the tree, he passed Eric’s glass past the branches and around the tree.

‘Don’t worry the bottle was sealed.’ Robbie said, as they chinked their glasses. They both had a sip of their drinks, before Robbie put his glass down and picked up the lights cable where he had left it before threading it back around to Eric.

‘Cheers.’ Eric said as he took the cable back off Robbie, ‘if your theory is correct, then we would need to ensure that the murderer did not find out that we knew there had been a murder.’

‘Obviously.’ Robbie replied.

‘Well what about the note?’

‘Ooh crap, that’s a good point. One of us should get it.’ Robbie said.

‘Well I can’t imagine anyone would have gone in there, even the killer knows Robert is dead because Patricia said the next morning.’

‘Ok, well we should get it just in case?’ Robbie queried.

'Probably, the killer might want to go back to make sure they left no clues.'

'Right, but how do we get in?'

'You could ask my aunt for keys?'

'No thank you buddy, then she'll know we're in there, we still don't know if you aunt didn't do it.' replied Robbie.

'Don't be daft; anyway just don't accept a drink off her if that was the case. I'm sure in hand to hand combat, we should be able to overpower my aunt.'

As Eric finished his sentence, Joe walked into the room carrying a tray. He looked at Eric and Robbie draping the lights over the tree before moving to the other end of the room to place the tray down.

'Hey, why don't you ask Joe for some keys? He must have some as he's on reception.' Eric leaned around the back of the tree and whispered in a low voice to Robbie.

'You must be joking!' Robbie whispered quickly back, 'He's my number one suspect, I'm not walking round the place with him by myself.'

'Don't be stupid. Anyway I can ask him to help me with the tree, I will keep an eye on him here.' They continued to talk in hushed voices behind the tree whilst Joe continued to unload his tray.

'What if he attacks you?' Robbie asked.

'We have no reason to think he is the murderer, anyway if he tries anything, I'll clobber him with that bottle you just gave me.' Eric nodded towards the bottle he had sat next to him behind the tree, 'just run up there and come straight back down. You can put the note in your pocket, you'll be back here in a minute if you're quick. I'll just keep him talking.'

'No way, anyway how am I supposed to ask for a key without being suspicious?' Robbie whispered back.

'You'll think of something.' Eric smiled and looked up to see Joe approaching the door to leave. Joe saw the two of them looking and stopped.

'Your aunt thought you might both require some sort of refreshment after your travails this morning. There are some cold meats, bread, cheese, and chutneys.'

'That's great Joe, thank you.' Eric said. Joe nodded and put his hand towards the door, 'Joe! Is there any chance Robbie can have a key to

Robert's room?' Joe stopped and stood up straight looking at both of them stood around the tree. He looked at Robbie.

'Is there any reason you wish to access Mr Wilson's room? I think under the circumstances it may be better if we leave the door closed.'

'Yeah, well that's the thing.' Robbie looked at Eric and then back to Joe, he felt a sudden flush of warmth come to his face. 'We, umm, I need to - '

'He has left his phone in there, plus I was going to suggest to Patricia that we open the windows to make sure the room isn't too putrid when they come to take away the body.' Eric cut in. Joe stared at the both before replying.

'I didn't realise you had both been in there?'

'Yeah, Patricia asked if we could check if he had had a heart attack or not.' Robbie replied.

'Well I will go collect your phone and I can open the windows, I guess that probably does make sense.' Joe said.

'Na, don't be daft, pass me the keys, I will be back before you know it anyway.' Robbie moved away from the tree and approached Joe.

‘Anyway you can give me a hand with these lights whilst Robbie is gone.’ Eric said, holding up one end of the lights. Joe looked at them both before smiling slightly.

‘Ok, well I have the keys to the rooms currently in use on me now so you’re in luck.’ Joe said as he pulled out a large looking set of small keys from his pocket. He singled out one key with a small number on it, ‘I wouldn’t usually do this but considering I’m not supposed to be working today and I can’t really be bothered going upstairs I’ll hand them over.’ He said passing the keys to Robbie, holding them by the one key, which singled it out from the others, ‘Just be quick and bring them back, last thing I want today is Patricia breathing down my neck.’ Robbie took the keys and looked at Eric triumphantly before leaving out the wooden door.

‘Have you all got keys to every room?’ Eric asked, leaning forward to insinuate that Joe aid him with the lights.

‘No, just me and Katie.’ Joe moved forward to the tree and took the lights from Eric, ‘I think Patricia has a spare set elsewhere in case we ever lose ours but she doesn’t use them as far as I know.’

Robbie quickly crossed the reception room floor towards the door for the staircase taking him up to Robert’s room. There was nobody in the reception, but the quiet meant he could hear the whistle of the wind picking up outside. It was probably snowing he thought, *White Christmas indeed!* He thought to himself happily. He pushed his way through doors and was greeted by Mrs Fox coming down the stairs.

'Oh sorry, Hi.'

'Hello.' Robbie replied, quickly moving past her.

'You haven't seen my daughter downstairs in the lounge have you?' She asked turning around.

'No afraid not, I've not seen her.' Robbie turned and continued up the stairs. He left Mrs Fox at the bottom of the stairs before he heard the door close and he presumed she had continued her search for her daughter. Robbie jogged up the stairs and past the floor where he and Eric were staying, despite the fact that neither of them had actually spent the night in their rooms. Robbie was already starting to feel a little drowsy and could feel the urge for a nap in front of the fire coming on. He'll suggest that when they finish the tree, he thought to himself. He reached the next floor, the keys jangling loudly in his hand as he was still holding the set by the key which Joe had singled out for him as the key to Robert's room. He pushed his way through the door onto the corridor leading to Robert's room. He quickly moved along the corridor, the carpeted floor hiding any sound from his footsteps. He got to the room and pushed the key into the slot on the door handle and tried turning it but it wouldn't move in the slot. *Great* he thought, now he would have to check all the keys before he could get in. He pulled the key out and tried the door handle which to his surprise was unlocked. The key he had used had not twisted to open the door so the room must have been open. How careless he thought and he pushed the door open and walked into the room. The lights were on and Robert was still slumped over his desk unmoved. Robbie walked up to the desk but straight noticed that the letter was no longer underneath Robert's hand on the desk. Somebody had already been and taken the note. He heard a floorboard creak behind him. *Crap* he thought to himself, the last thing he remembered before he hit the floor.

'Tree is already looking pretty good.' Joe said standing back and looking at the lights as Eric clambered down from the tree. 'I'm already feeling more festive'

'Good!' Eric said laughing as he got down to admire the tree's lights. He thought Joe seemed a lot more relaxed from the stiff seeming character he had first met. ‘Well I guess you guys can relax from working now anyway?’

‘Yeah’ Joe shrugged, ‘I am sure Patricia will still expect to us do some work.’

‘Have a few drinks with us tonight, once she sees you relaxing, she won’t ask you to do any work in front of us anyway.’

‘Not sure she would dare anyway,’ Joe smiled, ‘I think I was probably a little over the top this morning when she explained the situation to me.’ Joe rubbed the back of his neck. ‘I do actually feel kind of bad now, I mean it’s not her fault the weather is bad.’

‘I know but I can understand, nobody wants to spend Christmas at work.’ Joe said.

‘It’s not even that, I don’t really have anywhere special to be and I don’t really embrace the festivities usually. I had planned a trip to Brazil to spend Christmas and New Year.’

‘Yeah, I heard about the planned trip.’ Eric said.

‘Well it happens and I think I will be able to get everything back with insurance. It was just like the first big trip away, and you know how you build them up in your head? I have been counting down to it for weeks. Seemed like a good way to get away from everything for a few weeks and just clear my head.' Joe looked at Eric.

'Well, let's just make the most of Christmas at the hotel then I guess?' Eric responded. Joe nodded in response without saying anything and he eyes reverted to looking back at the tree.

'Your friend has been gone for a long time.' Joe then said.

'I was just thinking the same.'

'I really can't do with the hassle of him losing that set of keys.' Joe looked at Eric, 'any chance we can go and see where he has got to?'

'Yeah, but don't you worry about it. I will go find him, knowing Robbie, he has probably found himself a drink somewhere. I'll go find him and return your keys.' Eric said and Joe answered with another of his silent nods. Eric headed out of the room and closed the door behind him, leaving Joe staring at the tree. He headed into the reception area and saw Katie walking in from the direction of the front entrance. She smiled at him.

'Have you seen Robbie mulling around anywhere?' He asked.

'I'm afraid not, maybe he is with the Fox's daughter?' She replied, but Eric looked back at her nonplussed. 'Mrs Fox has just asked me if I have seen her daughter. It's not that big a hotel, not sure how people keep losing each other.'

'I'm sure I'll track him down.' Eric replied.

'Good luck, wouldn't want anything to break up your comedy duo.' She said as she headed behind the reception desk. Eric left the reception via the stairs to the next floor, he bounded quickly up the stairs, starting to worry that maybe Robbie had come across someone with murderous intentions. He came out onto the corridor and immediately saw Robbie slumped sat against the corridor wall outside Robert's room, clasping his head.

'What's going on?' Eric asked as he quickly walked over.

'Some lunatic just cracked my across the back of my head.'

'What? When?'

'Just now in there.' He pointed back at Robert's door to his room. 'Plus the note has gone.'

'You alright?' Eric said, as he pushed Robert's door open. 'What happened?'

'Went in as we had planned, the note was already gone from the desk, next thing I know someone smashes me over the back of the head. Then I woke up feeling like crap on the floor. How long have I been gone?'

'Not that long, me and Joe finished the lights but you've haven't been gone that long.' Eric said, pulling Robert's door closed. 'Well at least we know it wasn't Joe, he has been with me the whole time.'

'Well I don't think it was him anyway, whoever it was wearing a lot of female perfume. It was the only thing I noticed before I was knocked out.'

'You think it was our murderer?'

'Must be, why else would anyone take the note and then smash me over the head. They obviously just didn't hit me hard enough.'

'Christ.'

'Let's go get me a drink; I've had enough of playing detective.' Robbie said as he pushed himself up to standing.' As they said that Joe came through the door from the stairs and looked at the two of them.

'What's going on?' He asked as he quickly paced over to the two of them. He quickly grabbed Robbie's arm as Robbie steadied himself to standing.

‘I’ve just been cracked over the head by somebody in Robert’s room.’ Robbie said rubbing the back of his head.

‘What?’ Joe said, ‘who was it? And why?’

‘I didn’t see them, I didn’t know they were in there, they hit me over the head from behind.’

‘Let me have a look.’ Said Joe. Robbie craned his head down and Joe head a look at the back of his head.

‘Is it bad? It feels sore.’

‘Well there is a cut but it’s not too big so you won’t need any stitches but you have a large bump on your head. You feeling nauseated at all?’

‘Don’t think so.’

‘Well let’s get you downstairs, we can sit you down and I’ll grab you a bag of ice to put on your head.’ Joe said.

They started down the corridor. Robbie still felt groggy but obviously he had got off lightly from whoever he had disturbed in the room.

‘What about the keys?’ Eric asked as they approached the door to the stairs.

Robbie looked at Eric and shook his head. 'They were gone when I came to. Whoever clattered me over the head now has keys to all the rooms in the house.'

'What are you two talking about?' Joe asked, holding the door open for Robbie to shuffle through.

Robbie and Eric exchanged glances, both of them trying to distinguish what they should say and how much they should reveal.

'We think that Robert might have been murdered.' Eric said.

'Murdered? Don't be ridiculous.' Joe replied immediately.

'It's true.' Robbie follow up. 'And I think whoever killed Robert might have been the person who just attacked me now.'

'What on earth? But why would they attack you? And what makes you think there has been a murder?' Joe has stopped at the top of the stairs, placing his hands on his hips, waiting for their explanation.

'Look, I know it sounds unbelievable, but we think Robert was murdered. That's why we have been wanting to call the police, but obviously we haven't been able to.' Eric said.

'But why do you think he was murdered?'

'He left a note. Pretty much telling us that he was about to be murdered.' Robbie said.

‘Did he not say by who? And should we be worried? Is there some crazed maniac running around the place?’ Joe was asking questions quickly.

‘He didn’t say who.’ Eric said, then looking at Robbie and back to Joe. ‘We don’t think anyone has got in since the snow started, so we think it might be one of the guests at the hotel.’

‘What did the note say?’ Joe asked immediately. Eric seemed a little caught off guard by the interest in the note, and it left him feeling rather suspicious of Joe. The tone with which he had said it suggested he was more concerned by the note than a potential murder in the hotel.

‘It just said that he felt that he and Patricia were in danger.’ Robbie said.

Joe stared at Robbie for a second before smiling. ‘You two are having me on.’

‘I wish we were.’ Robbie said, ‘why else do you think I got this knock? I was going to retrieve the note.’

Joe stared at the two of them; he seemed to be summing up whether to believe their story and was waiting to see if either of them would suddenly burst into laughter.

‘I know it seems like a joke, but we are genuinely telling the truth.’

Joe rubbed his brow, and looked up at the two of them. ‘Right I need to speak to Patricia.’

‘She already knows.’ Robbie said.

‘Goddamit, who doesn’t know? Right get yourself downstairs, I’ll grab you some ice and then I think we should let everyone know what is going on.’ With that Joe turned and quickly jogged down the stairs, leaving Eric and Robbie to take to the stairs themselves.

Eric listened to Joe’s footsteps getting fainter before he heard the door on the ground floor open and close. He turned to Robbie who was still tentatively touching the bump on the back of his head before examining his fingers for traces of blood.

‘Stop playing with it.’ Eric said. ‘Do you think we should have told Joe about the note?’

‘Why wouldn’t I have done?’ Robbie replied, ‘it wasn’t him who clocked me over the head or took the note.’

‘I know, but he seemed kind of interested in what the note said. Gave me a weird feeling.’

‘Well the note has gone, and anyway it isn’t him we should be worried about.’

'He was with me the whole time to be fair.' Eric replied.

'Not just that, whoever cracked me over the head was wearing women's perfume.'

'Perfume?'

'Yep, the only thing I noticed, but it was strong enough that I did notice.'

'Wow, so at least that narrows the field.' Said Eric, half speaking his mind aloud.

'And anyway, even if we are a little suspicious of Joe, I got one upper hand on him already.'

'What do you mean?' Eric asked.

Robbie stopped on the stairs and ruffled in his pocket before pulling out the keys and holding them up in front of Eric's face. 'I still have these.'

'I thought you said they'd gone.'

'I did but whilst I was sat outside that room, I had a little idea to make us all feel a little safer. Joe said there are three sets of keys in the hotel which open all the doors. Katie has a set, Patricia has an emergency set, and now I have the other set.' Robbie looked at Eric, ‘if we can get those last two sets of keys, we are then safe to stay locked in our locked rooms without anybody paying us a visit.’

Eric smiled at Robbie, ‘clever boy!’

Robbie gave a thumbs up and put the keys back in his pocket. As he did, his knee buckled under him slightly but Eric grabbed his arm.

‘Best get you sat down mate.’ Eric said.

‘I agree, and we can work out which of our mystery ladies has got our note.’

CHAPTER 5 – CHRISTMAS EVE

Robbie sat nursing his head with a bag of frozen veg and in the other hand he held a small glass of whisky from which he was taking small sips. The light coming through the windows was getting darker as the early winter nights rolled in but Eric had switched on the tree lights which twinkled around the darkening room, giving off a warm glow. Joe was arranging wood on the fire to warm up the room and despite the earlier events, Robbie was feeling satisfactorily merry. After coming downstairs, Robbie had stationed himself on the long sofa by the fire and watched as the rest of the guests scurried around.

Eric and Joe had decided to go speak with Patricia, rather nonchalantly leaving Robbie alone to nurse his wounds which he had not appreciated, and then they had decided amongst themselves to tell the other guests. Katie obviously already knew, so she and Patricia had gone to Kailey, and the Fox's rooms to fill them in on what had happened. Joe meanwhile had told Brian, so now all the guests knew of the circumstances in the hotel. In a daze of hearing loud voices, slamming doors, accusations, and tears, Robbie had sat back and enjoyed his warming drink, and had started to feel quite festive with the smell of the pine needles.

'Robbie!' Eric had leaned forward and was looking at Robbie. Joe also was turned from the fire looking at Robbie. 'Are you still with us? I have been talking to you' Eric said.

'Sorry mate, Yeah I'm good, just enjoying the ambiance.'

'Ambiance? They must have hit you hard over the head. I think everyone is coming down now anyway.' Eric said.

The fire sparked a tiny flame which crackled some of the wood, and Joe leaned back, 'there we go. We'll get this place nice and cosy.' He smiled to himself and then at Eric and Robbie. As he said this, a small commotion could be heard from the hall, as the room door opened and Kailey and Katie walked in. They themselves were locked into a conversation.

'…how couldn't you have told anybody? Neither of you had the right to hold that kind of information from the rest of us.' Kailey was remonstrating.

'We felt at the time it was the best thing to do, as we weren't sure of anything.' Katie was appealing to Kailey, who had pushed past her and towards the drinks.

'What's up?' Eric asked.

Katie rolled her eyes before Kailey turned quickly around. 'What's up? What do you think is up? The fact that you all decided to keep the secret that there was a murder in the hotel.' Kailey had picked up a bottle before putting it down and grabbing a sealed one herself which she carried over to the chairs with her.

'We -' Eric started.

'Don't start with that *we thought it would be the best for you not to worry* you had no right in making that decision. Plus the Foxs can't find their daughter, so what if she has also been taken by our 'killer'' She said making inverted commas with her fingers.

‘They can’t find their daughter?’ Joe asked quietly, ignoring the angst of Kailey. She silently shook her head back at him, and with it her anger dissipated as she sank back into her chair.

‘They were looking for her earlier but they had presumed she had stormed off because she was unhappy spending Christmas at the hotel. Obviously under the circumstances, they are a little more worried now.’ Katie said.

‘Should we go help?’ Robbie asked.

‘You can’t go anywhere.’ Eric said directly to Robbie, ‘but yeah, maybe we should all split up and check the hotel.’

‘We have already checked every room.’ Katie said. ‘Mr Fox, is about to go search outside, but he is still giving Patricia a piece of his mind.’

‘I’ll go help, I don’t see why he can be angry at me, I was just as in the dark as he was?’ Joe said.

‘I’ll come too, surely the more of us the better.’ Eric said. Joe nodded, and he, Eric, and Katie exited the room. Robbie looked at Kailey who sat staring into the distance but he decided against initiating a conversation and the frown on her forehead was still faintly visible, so he watched the fire as it began to grow and continued sipping his drink.

In the main reception, Mr and Mrs Fox were still stood confronting Patricia as the others joined them. Mr Fox turned round as they approached and Eric could see the anger behind his glare so decided to leave the talking to Joe.

'We're going to help you look around outside.' Joe said as they reached the Foxs. 'You can remonstrate all you want later, but the thing is to find you daughter, once we have found her, you can yell at whoever you want.' Mr Fox stared at Joe as if he was preparing to continue his verbal attack but Joe's words sunk in and he nodded.

'Just stay here, we can just spread out and look for footprints around the hotel. If we don't find any, we will know she is somewhere inside the hotel.' Mr Fox said to his wife in a conciliatory manner. He turned to the others, 'I'll go fetch my coat and we can head outside.'

'No need, Robbie is staying here, his coat is there so just use that.' Eric pointed towards the door. Mr Fox glared back at Eric but then headed towards the door. Eric, Joe, and Katie followed towards the hotel door. Eric could see through the window that the sky was now dark, and what little moonlight remained was blocked by clouds, leaving little light to see past the glow of lights emanating from the hotel.

The group headed into the night and the icy breeze of the evening hit them all as soon as they stepped outside. The snow had stopped, but the temperature had fallen, and the snow has iced over, so each footstep crunched as it broke the crystallised snow. They looked to Mr Fox for instructions before, he looked past the group and ran steps into the distance. Eric looked in the direction he had gone, and saw a huddled younger Fox making her way back towards the hotel. He could hear the raised voices of jubilation and anger coming from Mr Fox, but the whistle of the wind drowned out the words. It sounded like relief mixed with anger. They came back towards the group, Mr Fox had his arm round his daughter.

'Oh thank goodness' Katie said. Mr Fox did not respond but his daughter gave a meek smile to Katie. They pushed past and towards the door, and the rest followed. They overheard the jubilation from Mrs Fox, as they re-entered the hotel. Eric walked in to see Mrs Fox hugging her daughter and rubbing her cheeks whilst smiling in joy.

'Where on earth have you been?' She asked her, 'you're ice cold.'

‘It’s nothing to worry about, I was tired of being here so I went to try and get a phone signal.’ She replied rather defiantly, ‘I wouldn’t have gone if you hadn’t trapped me here over Christmas.’

‘For goodness sake Stephanie, you could have gotten lost and frozen to death.’

‘Don’t be so dramatic dad, I was gone about an hour.’ She replied. ‘Anyway I didn’t get a signal so I came back again. Can we please just go home?’

Mrs Fox looked at Mr Fox and then at her daughter. ‘As soon as this snow clears we will leave.’ She said smiling.

‘Really?’ Stephanie asked. She turned from her mother to Mr Fox, who nodded and smiled. The complexion and attitude of the family had completely changed and for a moment, Eric completely forgot that there had been a murder at the hotel. He decided to go back and have a drink with Robbie.

‘Thanks for offering to help.’ Mr Fox said to the others, ‘I guess I was just worried with what has happened etc.’

‘Don’t worry, I would have been exactly the same.’ Katie said, ‘why don’t you come join us in the main room, I think we are all going to make the most of it being Christmas eve?’

‘That sounds lovely.’ Mrs Fox had stepped forward and answered for her husband. ‘We best get this one warmed up, and then we’ll come down.’

‘I’ll get Brian to make you both a hot chocolate, that should do the trick.’ Patricia said from behind the group.

‘Thank you.’ Mrs Fox smiled and went off with her daughter towards the stairs.

‘Mrs Bradshaw, I-’ Mr Fox started.

‘Please, no reason to apologise for anything. If anything I should be apologising for not making clear what had happened sooner.’ She cut in, ‘let’s just enjoy the rest of the evening, come down and join us for a drink and some Christmas festivities.’

‘Ok we will do.’ He said, and then he turned to Eric, ‘oh before I forget, I found this in your friend’s jacket pocket. I took it out when I found Stephy as it was rather uncomfortable and forgot to give it back.’ He handed Eric a large smooth paperweight.

‘Er, ok thanks, I’ll give it back to him.’ Eric took the large round shape and noticed its weight.

‘You will not give it him, that’s one of the paperweights from the guest rooms. Why on earth did your friend have that with him?’ Patricia said.

‘I haven’t a clue.’ Eric said, ‘first I have heard of it.’

‘Really Eric, who are you bringing into the hotel?’ Patricia said.

‘I don’t think he stole it Auntie, I don’t think he has even been in his room yet.’

‘He probably took a shine to it in your room or Robert’s’ She replied.

‘I’ll ask him.’ Eric walked back to the large room where he had left Robbie and Kailey. Patricia followed behind, Joe and Katie remained in the main hall, perhaps wanting to avoid any more animosity in the hotel. They walked into the room and Robbie looked up.

‘Any news?’

‘Yeah, she’s fine, she had gone to look for a phone signal.’ Eric replied. ‘Robbie - ’

‘That’s good news then. I knew she’d been fine, and to be honest one of us should have tried getting a signal. I guess she didn’t get one?’ Eric shook his head and held up the paperweight.

'It's hardly good news then is it?' Kailey said. 'I mean the fact of the matter is we are still stuck here without a signal and with a murderer. You all seem to be taking it strangely well.'

'Robbie, is this - ' Eric tried again as he held up the paperweight.

'We aren't completely sure there has been a murder and even if there was, the murderer may have already left.' Robbie replied directly to Kailey.

'Robbie, is this your paperweight?' Eric quickly said.

'You can't guarantee whether the murderer has left or not!' Kailey said. Robbie looked confusingly at Eric, and then back to Kailey.

'No you're right I can't but there is no use getting worked up. And what are you on about Eric?' Robbie said, confusion etched on his expression.

'Mr Fox, found this in your coat pocket.' Eric held the paperweight back up.

'Mate I haven't got a clue what you're talking about or what that is.' Robbie replied, standing up to move towards Eric and his stretched out arm.

'Did you take the paperweight from Robert's room?' Patricia asked abruptly.

'Paperweight? Why would I take a paperweight?' Robbie still seemed confused by the line of questioning. 'Are you suggesting I stole it? Even if I was a thief, which I'm not, I wouldn't steal something as pointless and ugly as a paperweight.'

Patricia eyeballed Robbie, before letting out a sigh and turned to leave the room. Robbie looked at Eric confused.

'Sorry mate, I think the whole thing is getting to her. More interestingly, I was trying to work out why this was in your coat pocket. Then Auntie mentioned Robert's room. What if this is the object that clubbed you over the head?' Eric said. Kailey's interest peaked at this point and she too got off the sofa to go and inspect the paperweight.

'That means it might have fingerprints on for the police to check?' Kailey asked.

'I guess so.' Robbie said, answering both their questions at once.

'Well I have been holding it, and so was Mr Fox. Plus if the staff don't clean their paperweights thoroughly it could have hundreds of guest's fingerprints on it.' Eric said.

'Why would they have put it in my coat?' Robbie asked.

'Maybe they were rushing and it was the easiest place to put it?' Eric replied.

'I think you should put it down somewhere safe. You never know the police might be able to find something useful off it?' Kailey said.

Eric agreed and put it on one of the bookshelves behind him.

'Not exactly Fort Knox.' Robbie said.

'Nobody will be looking for it, and we're all going to be in this room this evening anyway.' Eric said, and he moved to sit down. 'I for one suggest that we chill out in here all together and we should all be safe as houses.'

Robbie stared at the bookshelf as the other two sat down before turning to join them, 'Whatever happens, I'm taking that paperweight when we get out of here.'

As the evening went on, the atmosphere of the hotel lifted and the guests soon forgot about the events over the last few days. Even Kailey began to relax; the Foxs joined them in the main room, and poured themselves drinks. Joe and Katie came to join them, both refraining from drinking but joined in the conversations. After preparing more mince pies and warm sandwiches, Brian eventually joined the group. The guests had decided against a proper meal and unanimously decided that the hotel's chef join them to enjoy Christmas Eve rather than cook all evening. Patricia had come and placed small stockings above the fire which hung decoratively below the garland laced mantelpiece. The snow had begun to fall again, but with less animosity and it gently fell outside the window which led Katie and Eric, much to Robbie's delight, to admit it looked like it would be a White Christmas. Patricia had put on traditional carols and the music was a nice backdrop to the guests talking and the crackle of the fire. Eric has stayed quiet for the most part of the evening as he used the opportunity to work through the guests and what had unfolded. He had reached the conclusion that the most likely occurrence was that someone outside the group of guests had killed Robert and that Patricia was most likely still a target if said person had decided to stick around. However the search for Stephanie Fox had revealed no signs of someone living unbeknown to the staff in the hotel and it was unlikely anyone had been outside the whole time. The fact that the murderer had not made sure that Robbie was dead when he was attacked suggested the murderer was not a ruthless killer but rather someone with a motive to kill Robert and Patricia but he could not see any motives in the guests sat around the fire. The notion that disgruntled staff had committed the murder seems farfetched and none of them had shown outright animosity towards Patricia. Joe who had come closest was arguably more dismayed at having to work through Christmas, whereas Katie seemed to have a friendly relationship with her boss. He could only account for himself and Robbie when Robert was found, but the poison, if it was poison, could have been given to Robert at any stage in the evening. He looked at the females sat around the room, and thought about Robbie's comment that he had smelt a strong smell of perfume but he could not see any of the guests having the motive for wanting Robert and Patricia dead. Unless Robert's death was accidental? He decided that his attempts at playing detective were futile as he had very little to go on, and he was not in a position that he could question any of the guests of their whereabouts. He decided the best approach was to make sure his aunt, himself, and the rest of the guests stayed alive until the snow cleared. Keeping them all together was his first step in his plan and so far had worked rather well with the ambiance of the room remaining cheerful throughout the evening. Whoever the killer was, they would struggle to overpower the whole group if they stayed together, and whilst the snow drifts were still high, they would melt eventually, so it was a case of keeping the group together.

'Brian, these mince pies are unbelievable mate.' Robbie said to Brain across the room, raising his half eaten mince pie. Brian nodded in appreciation, raising his glass, as Robbie continued, 'considering the circumstances we're in, I'd say this was a perfect Christmas setting.'

'Not for me' Kailey said.

'Nor me.' Said Joe

Robbie rolled his eyes at both of them. 'What would you consider better than this? The drinks, the tree, which I add me, Eric, and Joe decorated superbly, the fire, the old country hotel setting. The snow!' He added at the end.

'The body' Kailey added quietly.

'Ok, well that isn't perfect but that aside, it's nice we're all spending Christmas Eve together.' Robbie smiled around the room, 'even our resident moody teenager seems a little happier.' He said smiling at Stephanie. She smiled back as did her parents; the joviality in the room had certainly improved thought Eric.

‘Still not my ideal Christmas.’ Kailey said but more light heartedly this time. She had refrained from drinking and still remained the most astute of the group but she was starting to talk a little more.

‘Go on then, let’s hear your ideal Christmas.’ Robbie said, ‘and then you Joe, as you seem so miserable by it all.’

‘Well,’ Kailey started, ‘I don’t see the appeal of all the clichés which seem to have caught your eye. I find the whole thing dreary, the endless attempts to sell everything which has a price on it, I find it quite relieving come January.’

‘Well that was Scrooge’s answer. How about you Joe?’

‘I’m not a huge fan either.’ He held up his hand to stop Robbie’s remonstrations, ‘but I have to admit, this is all very cosy. But there is a reason why I had planned on going to Brazil over Christmas, the weather for a start! And yes I know we have deep white snow outside but we usually have cold and rain and the nights are long, so I find it all a little depressing.’

‘Good point.’ Eric said.

‘Well I have to agree with Robbie.’ Mrs Fox said. ‘I was expecting the worst Christmas ever earlier today, but what beats this? Everyone talking and smiling, a warm fire, a magnificent tree. This is exactly what I planned when we decided to come.' She said smiling.

'I've actually been here at Christmas before.' Kailey said

'Really? When?' Eric asked.

'A couple of years ago, I guess? I'm afraid I gave your aunt an awful review for the place but it does look a lot nicer this year.'

'I don't remember you being a guest.' Katie said, 'I think I've been here 3 years maybe?'

'Oh well, I was here, maybe it was before you started.' Kailey said smiling back at Katie. Her response was curt in the way she delivered it, and Eric couldn't decide whether she was annoyed at Katie's checking of details or whether she was covering something. At that second, Patricia walked in the room, with a large Christmas stocking in her hand, smiling.

'Now I know it's rather random, so I apologise for the quality of the presents, but I got you all a little something. We all seemed so content this evening that I thought it was be a nice time to pass them around.' She smiled at the room, and there was a chorus of thanks as she began to hand out the small Christmas presents wrapped so delicately. She moved over towards Eric. 'I am afraid I do not have a gift for your friend, I wasn't aware he was coming.'

'Don't worry about it Auntie, but will you please stay in this room? We don't know what is going on in the hotel so I don't think it is safe for you to be wrapping Christmas presents by yourself.' She shooed his comment away with a flick of the hand and continued passing presents around. The group all starting unravelling the wrapping around their small gifts as they revealed small bottles of alcohol, sweets, joke books, they were small gifts but it further lifted the mood, especially as Joe began reciting jokes in his dry manner. Patricia took a seat and joined the rest of them.

'I do apologise Robbie, you would have received a gift also if Eric hadn't neglected to inform me you were coming.' Patricia said.

'No problem at all, looks like we're in the same boat anyway as you don't have one either.'

'I prefer giving presents that receiving so never you worry.' She said with a smile.

'Well we can do it again next year, hopefully in better circumstances, and maybe keep our presents under the tree.' Katie said.

‘There is something under the tree.’ Kailey said pointing, and some of the guests turned their heads to look. A small wrapped gift was underneath the tree.

‘Who left that?’ Eric asked.

‘Santa?’ Robbie offered looking for a smile but he didn’t receive one in return from anyone.

‘Well it wasn’t me. Eric go see if it has a name on it.’ Patricia said.

Eric got up from his seat and walked over to the tree. He could smell the pine smell coming from the freshly placed tree. He bent down and picked up the present which was wrapped in the same paper as the gifts that his aunt had just handed out but it was larger and heavier than the other gifts.

‘You sure it’s not one of yours auntie?’ He asked as he stood up holding the gift.

‘Course not, I’m not senile.’

‘Does it say anything?’ Katie asked, the rest of the guests were now looking and interested in the mysterious present. Eric turned it over and found a small label attached.

‘It’s for you auntie.’ Eric said and walked over handing her the gift.

'Well, I certainly didn't give the gifts out to receive anything in return, but whoever got me the gift, thank you very much.' She said smiling around the room, and she carefully began to unwrap the present with the rest of the guests all watching her. Eric looked around the room and everyone was intently watching apart from Stephanie Fox but she seemed rather bored by the present giving so was hardly a surprise. Patricia pulled a picture frame out of the wrapping and looked at it rather puzzled. She then looked rather angry, 'is this somebody's idea of a joke? I would have thought with everything going on, this was a rather low form of humour.'

'What is it auntie?' Eric asked, as Katie leaned over next to Patricia.

'It's an old photo from the school I used to work at.'

'There are crosses through some of the faces.' Katie said.

'Yes thank you Katie, no need to give whoever did this any kind of satisfaction.' She pulled the frame to her chest and begin to cover it back up with the wrapping looking angrily at Katie.

'Let me see auntie, it could be related to what happened with Robert.' Eric said.

'Don't be so ridiculous! It's just a childish joke and ill-mannered and crass.' She stood up and took the present with her and left the room.

‘Wow, that went down badly.’ Robbie said.

‘Did you do it?’ Katie asked angrily.

‘Course I didn’t. Where would I get an old school photo of her? I only met her yesterday.’ He retorted.

‘You’ve been in here all evening; you must have at least seen who left it.’ Kailey said. Robbie shook his head and shrugged his shoulders.

‘What was in the picture?’ Joe asked Katie and everyone looked at her.

‘Well I only saw it for a second, but it was a regular school class photo, but there were about 4 red crosses through some of the children’s faces, and a circle around Patricia.’ Katie said. ‘I couldn’t really see as she pulled it away so quickly.’

‘Do you think it has anything to do with Robert?’ Mrs Fox asked with a grief stricken face.

‘I’m sure it is someone’s idea of a joke to scare Patricia. I think we are all jumping to conclusions a little.’ Joe said trying to calm Mrs Fox.

‘Very easy for you to say, everyone said everything would be fine earlier when you all knew that Robert had been murdered.’ Kailey piped in reverting to her hysterical manner from earlier in the day.

‘Don’t accuse me; I knew nothing about the murder until you did.’ Joe retorted.

‘Yes but she did.’ Kailey pointed at Katie.

‘This is stupid, I’m going to my room, I will see you all in the morning.’ Brian had been reflective and quiet all evening so this outburst took everyone by surprise but before anyone challenged him, the chef had left the room and slammed the door behind him.

‘Not sure we should all be splitting up like this.’ Robbie said.

‘Why?’ Mrs Fox asked cautiously.

‘I’ll go after him.’ Katie said and smiled at the room before also leaving. The room fell into a silence apart from the crackle of the fire and the faint Christmas easy listening tunes which Robbie had put on earlier.

‘Can somebody please turn off that ridiculous music?’ Mr Fox said angrily. Robbie was going to argue but it happened to be passing through a bagpipe solo of *O Holy Night* so he thought better of it and leaned behind his seat, stretching to turn the music off. Eric’s plan to keep the guests together had quickly eroded following the gift to his aunt and the tensions had quickly arisen again. As he was preparing to calm down Mr Fox, Patricia slowly walked back into the room; she had a crestfallen face and was still clutching the present to her breast.

'You ok auntie?' Eric asked as the other guests stared at her. She nodded and sat down with a heavy sigh.

'I apologise, I shouldn't have stormed out, I was just a little shocked, and when I got outside I realised you all had a right to see the picture. Especially after keeping you all in the dark regarding Robert.' She looked imploringly at the Fox family.

'I think we all have a right to know what is going on under the circumstances.' Mr Fox said, more addressing the room than Patricia directly, like he was seeking approval. He received none as the lowly figure of Patricia had moved most of them to sympathy.

'What is it Patricia?' Joe said, cutting a glance at Mr Fox.

'Should I go and get Katie and Brian?' Robbie ventured. Patricia gave a wave of the hand and a weary smile in response.

'I will fill them in after. Unfortunately, I think that Robert's untimely death may have been a murder and that I may have brought this horrid affair upon you all.' She said.
'What do you mean auntie?' Eric asked, 'you can't blame yourself for any of this.' He continued, this last comment received a snort of derision from Kailey. Patricia didn't hear but Eric did but he ignored her input.
Patricia sighed heavily and passed Eric the photo frame. 'It's a photo of my old school; you can see me at the back of the picture.' Eric looked at the photo and his aunt was unmistakably in the photo, looking younger but sterner than ever in the face. 'It is a photo of one of my classes, why this class I have no idea.' She was talking whilst looking down at her lap, addressing herself more than anybody directly but the guests were all concentrated on her. Eric passed the photo to Joe as the photo went around the room. 'I have been trying to think what distinguishes this group of boys more than any of the other hundreds I taught but as you can see in the photo, it appears as if somebody has been targeting the children in this photo.' She looked up at the guests, 'I say children, these will all be grown

men now, including Robert who is the face which has been crossed out on the far left.'

'How can you know its Robert auntie? This could just be an attempt to scare you.' Eric said in a comforting voice.

'Oh I wish it was. You see at first I thought it was something stupid too and a ridiculous joke. But I have looked at the other faces crossed out on the photo. They're all dead.'

'The other three crossed out children are dead too?' Robbie asked.

'I'm afraid so.' She replied.

'Auntie this doesn't mean anything serious, anybody could have found this out and then done this to scare you after hearing about Robert.' Eric said.

'Nobody knows about Robert apart from us guests.' Joe said solemnly as he passed the photo on.

'I only realised that maybe this was serious when I remembered about the other children. I don't really keep in contact from anybody at the school. George our handyman at the hotel is the only remnant I have from those days but I try and keep in touch with people as I can but people get old, move on with their lives, and lose touch.'

'The guy who lives in that shed on the premises used to work at this school?' Robbie asked. Him and Eric exchanged glances.

'He did, we always stayed in touch and when we came here I trusted him to do what he did in the school. Obviously he was just a caretaker then so he's not in the photo.' Patricia continued. 'But I do still hear from old students. One of the pupils from a few years before this one is a CEO of some big biscuit company now and does very well for himself, they all seem to be dotted around different professions.' The guests continued listening to Patricia's story. Even Kailey seemed immersed in the tale. 'The thing is, you do hear about deaths as well, and for some strange reason the deaths seem to be much more frequently passed around via gossip than the achievements of other pupils. It's a sad affair but I suppose that is how society is nowadays, especially in rather macabre matters.'

'What happened?' Eric asked. The rest of the guests were leaving Eric to gently deal with his aunt as he slowly drew the story out of her.

'Well they are just random accidents really but seeing this photo makes me think that something a lot more sinister has happened.'

The photo had made its way back round to Patricia as she rested it on her lap. Even the Fox's had had a look, Mr Fox keeping it away from his daughter. 'About two or three years ago, George had told me that one of the pupils had been skiing with his family and was killed crashing off course, he was the boy in the middle of the frame crossed out.' She pointed at the frame more for herself than anyone as nobody could now see it rested on her lap. 'then I read about another, Raymond Williams, who had slipped and fallen climbing one of the mountains in Cumbria, they even said it was strange in the newspaper article because he was a seasoned climber and walker and the weather had been fine, they decided he must have fainted and toppled over the edge.'

'Mrs Bradshaw these all sound like terrible accidents, somebody is obviously trying to scare you.' Joe said.

'What about the last cross?' Robbie asked.

'I think we should maybe let Mrs Bradshaw be.' Joe answered Robbie.

'No, don't worry Joe, I am ok, I guess I may as well tell all I have to know and then at least we know I have been honest with you all.' Patricia said, and Joe nodded. Eric was perturbed at why Joe seemed to snap at Robbie but maybe he was genuinely concerned for his aunt. 'The last boy, Gerald, I remember him well, he was always so quiet and shy, I'm not sure he ever got on with the rest of the children, but he was ever so smart. That's the strange thing, the other boys were always together but Gerald wasn't even part of their friend circle so why anyone would want to hurt him as well as the others.'

'That's if they are attacking this class auntie, don't forget.' Eric said.

'I know, it could be all a coincidence but I saw about five years ago now, the first of all of them I think, Gerald had been found in his study at his family home, he had committed suicide.' She raised her hand before anyone said anything, 'yes I know, suicides, accidents, it is hardly evidence, but everyone said that Gerald's death was so out of the blue, he had a family, a good job, and no signs before that anything had happened. I think Robert had even kept in touch with him and went through a terrible depression after he heard the news.'

'This is absolutely ridiculous.' Mr Fox said abruptly, even Patricia raised her head. 'Suicides, accidents, murder, it's an elaborate fairy tale concocted from no evidence to suggest anything of the sort. I will not sit around here whilst you all fantasise you are acting out some Agatha Christie story. None of you are trained doctors so we don't even know if your friend was murdered anyway.' Everybody around the room looked at Mr Fox but none offered any repost, possibly as his words could certainly ring true, they had little to suggest bar an ill-timed photo to link anything to what had happened upstairs, Eric thought. Mr Fox stood up, 'I am going to my room, I don't expect to be disturbed for anything until tomorrow morning whereas I will be collecting some breakfast and then we shall remain in our family room until the snow has cleared enough for us to leave this ridiculous establishment.' His face was red, but his gusto had enlivened his wife who now stood up by his side. 'Really Mrs Bradshaw, I can understand the others playing detectives together but you really should know better, I came here to discuss finances with you over the holidays, not partake in some murder mystery dinner!.' With that he held his wife's hand and the two departed, Stephanie Fox giving a hurried if embarrassed smile as she followed quickly after them.

'Maybe he is right.' Patricia said, still sounding rather glum.

'Well, it certainly is a lot of coincidences.' Robbie said, 'you are right to at least wonder, especially after receiving that frame.'

'Auntie, who else would possibly know about that photo?' Eric asked.

'What do you mean?' Asked Patricia.

'Well is there anybody you still know from the school? Any grudges? Anybody you still keep in touch with?'

'Not really, nobody close enough anymore. Apart from George obviously but he hasn't mentioned anything.' She said thinking aloud.

'Auntie, you don't think George has anything to do with this?' Eric asked.

'Don't be ridiculous, I have known him for about 35 years.' She quickly responded, some of the fire returning to her eyes.

'Not necessarily the murder auntie, but maybe the photo, maybe it was a joke which he hasn't been able to explain?' Eric said.

'Or maybe it's some kind of tribute?' Robbie said, 'weird kind of tribute but you never know.'

'Well I guess so.' Patricia said, 'I did think it was strange he never came to wish my Merry Christmas before he left.'

'You never saw him go?' Joe asked. 'Me and Katie didn't either. We were saying it was strange as he seems so fond of Katie, we had bought him a small gift too.' Patricia shook her head in response to Joe.

'He wasn't at the shed when we went down and the place had been turned over.' Robbie said.

'So this George guy might still be lurking around the place? Even in the hotel??' Kailey said rather hysterically, she had obviously been following the conversation despite staring absent minded into the fire. 'Does he have keys??' she asked staring at Patricia.

'Well yes but you can't be suggesting something so preposterous.' Patricia answered.

'Since when did you decide what was preposterous or not? Because of your silly assumptions, we may have all been living inside this house with a murderer!' Kailey got up and stormed out of the room.

'You don't think? I mean I have known George for so long.' Patricia said meekly.

'I will go calm her down; nobody should be out and about like this whatever the circumstances. I will let her cool off and then make sure we both come back here. Whatever everyone thinks, I think staying here together is the safest option.' Joe smiled at Patricia and then followed after Kailey.

‘I don’t think this Christmas could have gone any worse.’ Patricia said, ‘I am terribly sorry you’ve come up here and got stuck in all this mess.’

‘Don’t be silly auntie, there is no reason to suspect that you have caused any of this, remember?’ Eric said trying to comfort his auntie, he looked at Robbie and had an expression pleading his help. Robbie shrugged and then leaned over and turned the soft Christmas music back on. He smiled in reply and Eric rolled his eyes. ‘Why don’t we all go together and make a cup of tea?’

‘I think I could do with something stronger tonight, Robbie will you please pour me a glass of whatever you are drinking?’ Patricia said.

‘My pleasure.’ Robbie jumped up to get a glass, felt rather shaky on his legs still either from the bang on his head or his own consumption and collected a glass for Patricia before sitting down and pouring a glass from the bottle he had placed under his seat. He leaned over with the glass and passed it to Eric who passed it to his aunt.

‘Thank you.’ She said meekly. ‘If it was George -’

‘Auntie don’t start thinking about that again.’ Eric said. She looked at him before continuing.

‘If it was George, why would he do this and where could he be?’

‘You know him better than us auntie.’ Eric said.

‘And he has a pick of the rooms in a hotel.’ Robbie added.

‘Yes but he doesn’t have keys for every room so he wouldn’t be able to hide away like that. He wouldn’t really have anywhere to hide. That’s what I find confusing; one of us wandering around the place would have seen him by now.’ She said.

‘What if he has some keys?’ Robbie asked. He touched his pocket lightly feeling the outline of the keys he had taken earlier in the day.

‘Well Katie and Joe have a set each, and then I have a set in my room. Unless one of those two have lost their keys or given them to George, he won’t be able to access any rooms.’ Patricia said looking at Robbie and then Eric.

‘Well why don’t we go and check your room? If we see the keys, and ask Katie and Joe for theirs, we will know that he definitely isn’t in any of the rooms.’ Eric said.

‘I can’t see him staying outside either so I think if the keys are still there then we can cross George off our list.’ Robbie said.

‘Quite right too. I don’t even like entertaining the thought but we can go check.’ Patricia said. ‘Boys, I may as well tell you everything I know. I want you both to be careful.’

‘Obviously auntie.’ Eric said and Robbie nodded.

‘It’s not that, its Katie -’ Patricia started but was broken off as a scream was heard echoing through the hotel. ‘What on earth -’ Patricia started. But Eric and Robbie were already stood up.

‘Come on.’ Eric said to both as he headed towards the door.

CHAPTER 6 - CHRISTMAS EVE

The three of them rushed into the hotel reception and were met by Joe and Mrs Fox who looked like they had just arrived too.

‘What’s going on? Is everyone ok?’ Joe asked as they arrived.

‘Yeah, we’re fine, we just heard the scream.’ Eric said.

‘Do we know where it came from?’ Robbie added.

‘Not sure, I was here when it happened but I couldn’t place it.’ Joe said.

'It was definitely down here somewhere because I heard it coming down the stairs.' Mrs Fox added. As she did Mr Fox and Stephanie came rushing through the doors looking dishevelled.

'Oh god, Julia, I thought it was you who screamed. Are you ok?' Mr Fox said as he approached his wife.

'Yes yes darling, I'm fine.' She replied. Mr Fox gave her a hug and then looked at her, his expression changing.

'Where did you run off to?' He asked.

'Never mind that.' Joe said, 'if it wasn't one of us, who was it?'

'No sign of Katie.' Patricia added.

'Or Kailey' Robbie added. As he did, Brian walked into the room from one of the doors heading off towards the kitchens that neither Eric or Robbie had ventured down as yet. He looked surprisingly calm as he approached the group.

'Are you ok?' Mrs Fox asked.

'Yes of course, what's going on?' he asked seeming confused rather than calm thought Eric.

'Did you hear the scream?' Eric asked.

'Of course I did, I'm not deaf.' He replied curtly.

'Where did it come from?' Patricia asked. Brian shrugged in reply.

‘Where were you?’ Robbie asked.

‘In the refrigerator, in the kitchen.’ He answered, ‘why?’

‘I thought you had gone off to your room.’ Robbie said eyeing the chef.

‘Right let’s not start with any accusations. We are still missing Kailey and Katie.’ Joe said. The group looked around themselves; they all seemed quite startled by the realisation and at the same time wary of each other. Almost all of the guests had been at different places in the hotel Eric thought. Moreover, whilst Brian and Joe were with them now, of the two people missing, Kailey had been pursued by Joe, and Katie had gone looking for Brian. Eric looked at the two men who both had similarly calm expressions on their faces. As Eric was about to confront them regarding this, Kailey walked into the lounge from outside, shaking herself down. She looked up and saw the group of guests.

‘What’s going on?’ she asked worry resonating in her voice.

‘We heard a scream. We thought it might have been you.’ Mrs Fox said.

‘A scream? Oh god, what is going on here.’ She said, panic in her voice. ‘Is everyone ok?’

‘We don’t know yet, we can’t find Katie.’ Eric said. Kailey came towards the group and seemed frail in the way she was walking, like the fear was getting the best of her. Either that or her lack internet was giving her withdrawals.

‘Oh god, I hope she is ok. We need to get out of here, let’s just all go together, we can make it.’ She said pleadingly.

‘Where were you?’ Joe asked. ‘I came to look for you.’

‘I went outside; I wanted to see if we could get away from the hotel, and I think we can, the snow isn’t too bad. I don’t want to stay here any longer.’ She said hurriedly.

‘You were quick getting outside.’ Joe replied with which she gave no response. Eric began adding up the scenarios and locations of each of the guests when he heard the scream. Kailey appears to have either gone to her room and then outside or straight outside with the latter more likely within the time frame. That means Joe has been alone in the hotel since he left the room. Mrs Fox was on the stairs and appears to have left their room, so Stephanie and Mr Fox should have been in their room but he would have to check with Stephanie later on surreptitiously to see if her father had also left the room. Brian, despite saying he had gone to his room, was downstairs in the kitchen, and it was after him that Katie had gone searching. Katie was not there but they had no proof that she had been the one who had let out the scream, and the worst scenario was that George was lurking around the hotel somewhere.

‘Should we split up and try and find Katie? I would hate for something to have happened to her.’ Patricia said. Eric looked at his aunt but she gave him a knowing glance.

‘I agree, there must be a sign of her somewhere in this hotel and she could be hurt.’ Joe said.

‘I am not going anywhere of the sort, we are leaving.’ Mr Fox said.

‘I have told you before about this playing detectives and I will not be party to any of it.’ He almost spat his final words. ‘Come on both of you.’

‘Are you sure that’s safe?’ Robbie asked. Mr Fox looked at him.

‘Whatever do you mean?’ he asked.

‘Well we can’t be exactly sure where your wife was when we heard that scream.’ Robbie answered. Eric cringed at Robbie’s lack of subtlety but he was also intrigued to see how the Fox family reacted.

‘How dare you.’ Mrs Fox said, demonstrating anger that the woman had previously not insinuated she was capable of showing.

'You have just decided for us, I do not care what the rest of you do or what happens to you for the rest of the night but we are leaving.' With that, the three of them turned around and headed towards the stair well, the door banging behind them as they exited. Everyone looked at Robbie.

'Come on, I was just saying, and why was she out of her room?' He received no support from the others.

'Anyway, whatever happens to the Fox family, let us try and find Katie. Brian and Joe, are you two ok looking around down here? Us three can check the upper floors and then we can meet back here afterwards?' Patricia said. Joe and Brian looked at each other and shrugged.

'Sounds like a plan. Try and make sure you stick together.' Joe said.

'Where should I be?' Kailey asked.

'Do you want to come with us?' Eric asked.

'I'm not so sure, the killer seems to have something against you Mrs Bradshaw so I may be safer with the others.' She looked at Patricia, 'sorry, no offence intended.' She added.

'None taken my dear.' Patricia answered.

'Come on then. Let's get this done, sooner I am back in my room away from all you loons the better.' Brian added. He, Joe and Kailey headed off towards the kitchen from where Brian had come.

'Do you think splitting up was the right thing to do auntie?' Eric asked in hushed tones in case they heard.

'Well, I have been thinking whilst all this has gone on. I know you may think me senile, but I cannot believe George has anything to do with any of this, and if his shed was smashed up in the way you two describe then, I fear for his wellbeing more than anything.'

'What do you mean?' You think one of the guests is responsible?' Robbie asked.

'Precisely. I don't have a clue who or why any of them seem to have any inclination to kill as I do not know any of them from my school years, but they were all alone around the hotel when we heard Katie scream and I don't trust any of them particularly.' Patricia said.

'Don't forget auntie that Katie could have faked that scream, we don't know whether she is hiding in this hotel too.' Eric said.

'Indeed we don't. But you two were with me and I have no reason to suspect you Eric nor your friend so you two can come with me whilst we check to see if I still have my keys in my room.'

'Sounds like a plan!' Robbie said.

'What about Katie?' Eric asked.

'Well after you two deliver me to my room, we can discuss that depending on if we have keys or not.' Patricia answered. Eric nodded and they set off for the stairwell to head to Patricia's room.

When they reached the room and Patricia let them both in, they entered the room, whilst Patricia went off through another door. The room was more akin to an apartment than a hotel room, and it was clear that she had turned this into a residential area for herself. She returned back from the room she came with a set of keys in her hand.

'Exactly where I left them.' She said, 'which means that if it is George he is doing a good job of getting around the place without being seen.'

'It's looking less likely that it is him auntie. Let's just hope he's ok or that he headed home before all of this started.' Eric said.

'I guess we better head back downstairs.' Robbie said. 'The good thing is that we have two of the three sets of keys.' He said lifted the other keys from his pocket.

'Where did you get them?' Patricia asked.

'Joe lent them to me, so at least if worse comes to worst we could hide ourselves in our room, and just hope the murderer doesn't have the other set.'

'We should try find the other keys, which Katie should have, then nobody can creep into any rooms unwanted.' Eric said. He turned with Robbie as they moved to leave.

'I'm going to stay here.' Patricia said.

'Don't be silly auntie, we can't stay here the whole time.' Eric said.

'Not all of us, just me.' She said.

'Auntie, you'll be much safer coming with us.' Eric said and Robbie nodded in agreement.

'Look, I am not arguing nor am I running around this hotel like I'm in the Scooby doo gang. I am the only person with a key for this room, and I can barricade the door as best I can once you leave.'

'Auntie, it's not safe. What if someone tries to break the door down?' Eric said.

'Have you seen how thick this door is?' She said, 'nobody is coming through there. Plus I will push the desk or bed up behind it too.'

'Why don't we just stay here too then?' Robbie asked.

‘You two need to make sure those people downstairs are safe, most of them are as scared as we are.’ Patricia answered, ‘plus you two can stop whoever is doing this.’

‘And if we can’t?’ Eric said.

‘Or they stop us?’ Robbie added.

‘Then I will have to cross that bridge when I get to it. Now get going and go find Katie and her keys.’

‘Ok well we will be back soon auntie. Don’t open for anyone unless you know it’s us.’ Eric said. Robbie gave a rhythm knock on the door.

‘You hear that and it’ll be us and you can open the door.’ He said.

‘Can’t you just tell me it’s you?’ She asked with a smile.

‘Ok we can do that too.’ Robbie said.

‘We will be back soon auntie.’ Eric said assertively. His auntie nodded and closed the door behind them both. They heard the key turn in the lock and steps away from the door on the other side before they set off back downstairs.

As they arrived into the main lounge, they were in time to see the Fox family exiting through the front door. Mr Fox turned and gave a glare at the two of them before he heading outside following his daughter and wife.

'Should we lock the door?' Robbie asked.

'What do you mean?'

'Well if there is someone trying to get in, or any other guests exiting and entering, then maybe we should stop it happening.' He hooked the keys back out of his pocket.

'I guess so, run after them and ask if they are ok the doors are being locked. I don't think you'll get a friendly answer but at least they know then. Tell them to knock on the window if they decide to come back.' Eric said.

'Why I am doing it?' Robbie asked.

'I'll get the others and see if they have found Katie. Then we can meet back by the fire and we will just keep everyone there whether they like it or not.' He said. Robbie nodded and walked quickly off towards the main door in pursuit of the Foxs. Eric turned to his right and went through the door which led to the kitchens and breakfast room where the other group had gone in search of Katie. He pushed his way through into the corridor which led to the breakfast room where they had had breakfast earlier that morning. It felt like an eternity away. He thought he would check there afterwards as he knew two further rooms went off from that room. He moved further down the corridor to the kitchen. He pushed the kitchen door tentatively open and looked for a light switch. The illuminating moon shone through the window to the right of the door and bounced off the shiny metal surfaces of the different cooking appliances but the room was still cast in shadows. He found a switch and the lights flickered to life before lighting up the room. There was no point in shouting out as he could clearly see he was the only one in the room but he decided to walk around the side of the cooking cabinets in case of any sprawled out bodies. He walked around the side and found nothing but a clean floor which Brian obviously kept immaculately clean. He decided to leave and check the dining room but saw a door beside the fridge which he hadn't see at all at first. He moved over to the door and pulled down on the handle and pulled the heavy door open. Stairs down into the darkness. He stood at the top of the stairs and looked down, he could see no sign of any light switch and there was obviously no natural light down there. It must have been a pantry of some sort for the kitchen; he thought it was strange that there was no light switch close to the door as Brian would risk breaking his neck every time he came down for supplies otherwise. He turned to see if the light was on the other side, when he heard a rustle somewhere down in the darkness.

'Hello?' He said into the darkness. He received no reply but the rustle had abruptly stopped when he spoke. He turned around to head back into the safety of the kitchen, and seek safety in numbers but the door slammed shut in his face. Somebody has closed me in, his mind screamed.

'Hey!! I'm down here!' He banged at the door, and looked for a handle to open and push the door open but he couldn't find a handle on this side of the door. 'Hey!' He shouted again but heard nothing from the other side of the door.

'Eric?' A voice from the darkness said and he wheeled back around, his eyes straining to make out the face behind the voice, his heart was pumping quickly in his chest. 'Eric? Is it you? It's me Katie.'

'Katie?' he said softly into the darkness but he quickly composed himself as he couldn't be sure if he was any safer with Katie or not. 'I can't see a thing.'

'Come down the stairs. Reach your hand out, I'll come find you.' He heard her voice closer now. He steadily took one step at a time lowered himself down the stairs until he took a hard step on concrete and then lifted his arms out in the darkness looking for Katie. He finally felt her cold hand grab his, and she clutched his hand in the dark.

'Oh god, what happened? Are you ok? We all heard you scream and we feared the worst.' Eric said speaking quickly.

'I'm ok, well I think I might have broken my wrist or something as I can't move it, and I think my head is bleeding. Somebody pushed me down the stairs.' She said. 'I don't know if they were trying to kill me and it's all related or what but I felt the hand push me and then I woke up on the floor. I have been down here since. I didn't say anything when the door opened as I didn't know who it was.'

'We need to find a way out of here, everyone has gone off separately, whoever is doing this can pick everyone off one by one.' He said, he was still gripping Katie's hand but there was no light for his eyes to adjust so he couldn't even make out her shape.

'The door can only be opened from the outside and there is no way of seeing any other way out.' Katie said. 'Aside from banging on the door, there is little we can do.'

‘There must be something we can do. Let’s try feeling around best we can, we can stay together and if we find nothing then we will just sit and bang the door until somebody hears us.’

Robbie was waiting in the main lounge by the fire but was alone, he wasn’t sure where Eric had got to nor where any of the other guests were. He poured himself another drink from the bottle he had under his chair from earlier but he downed this drink in one go, warming his throat on and stomach on the way down. He sat down and stared at the Christmas tree glistening, he was trying to think what to do next, whether to go find Eric or wait here like he had said. At that moment, the door opened and Kailey walked into the room.

‘Oh.’ She said abruptly, ‘I didn’t know anybody was in here.’ She moved cautiously over to the seats opposite Robbie and stared at him throughout. ‘Where is everybody else?’ she asked. Robbie stared at her, she was acting strangely but it could be because she trusted Robbie just as little as her trusted her, or anybody else in the hotel.

‘I haven’t a clue, I’m waiting for Eric to come back from looking for you lot.’

‘Looking for us?’ she asked.

'Yeah, we came down from upstairs and nobody was here.' Robbie answered, 'well apart from the Fox family but they have left now.'

'They have left??'

'Yeah about 10 minutes ago.'

'Why didn't we all leave together? With them?' Kailey asked incredulously.

'I don't think they'll get far, not unless they stupidly keep going once they realise how difficult it is out there.'

'Still, it seems a better option that being stuck here.' She said, she seemed to ease up as the conversation went on.

'Where have you been? And where are Brian and Joe?' Robbie asked.

'Well we couldn't find Katie. Only took us about five minutes to check to be honest, as there is nowhere for her to hide, or be hidden, so we came back here together.' Robbie continued to look at her which prompted the further, 'I don't know where Brian or Joe are.'

'Right.' Robbie said rolling his eyes, 'I guess it's probably best it we wait here for them to get back.' He lent forward to pour himself a drink before a loud bang smashed at the window, making him jump.

'What the hell was that?' Kailey said panicked.

‘Beats me.’ He responded.

‘Well it was the window, aren’t you going to have a look? Kailey asked. Robbie stared back worryingly at Kailey.

‘Whoever it is roaming this hotel has already had a crack at me.’ Robbie said pointed at his head, ‘I’m not giving them another opportunity.’ As he said it, the window banged again, and he could hear the muffled voice of Mr Fox at the window. He got up and pushed past the Christmas tree and pulled the heavy drape back. He saw Mr Fox on the other side, the light from the room illuminated his face. Mrs Fox had her arm round her daughter who had her face buried in her hands.

‘Let us in.’ Mr Fox demanded, and Robbie closed the drapes and headed back for the front door. After unlocking the main door, Robbie pulled it open and the Fox family hurried back in.

‘What happened?’ Robbie asked, Kailey was now stood beside him as they felt the cold air gush in from outside.

‘Couldn’t you make it?’ Kailey asked. Mr Fox looked at them both and shook his head, his daughter and wife had already gone on ahead without stopping. Mr Fox’s face was solemn as he looked at the two of them.

‘We found a body.’

‘What?’ Kailey asked.

‘We didn’t get far, the snow was too deep but we pushed on a bit further but when we decided to turn back, the snow we trod down must have shifted as Stephanie stumbled over a hand out there.’ Mr Fox said.

‘Who’s body?’ Robbie asked.

‘I don’t know, it was just the hand, cold and stiff, sticking out the snow.’ Mr Fox looked in shock, ‘I’ve never seen a body before. What the hell is going on here?’

‘We don’t know.’ Robbie said, ‘I can’t find the others now either.’

Mr Fox looked at him, even more worried now, gone was the angry man who had stormed out the hotel.

‘What should we do?’ Kailey asked.

‘We’re locking ourselves in our room, my daughter is distraught and whoever is doing all this will have to come through me and my wife to get to my daughter.’ Mr Fox said.

‘Don’t you think, it’d be better if we all stuck together down here?’ Robbie asked, ‘strength in numbers?’

‘I thought you were doing that anyway, I get back and I find only two of you together, I think I’ll be safer in my room.’ Mr Fox responded, moving away from the other two. ‘I think you two would be safer in your rooms too, that is if you even trust each other.’ And with that he left headed towards the doors leading to the stairs, following after his family.

‘What now? Do we listen to him?’ Kailey asked.

‘I think we should stay where we were, I told Eric we’d meet there and I don’t think we should keep splitting up to find people.’ Robbie said. Robbie walked with Kailey back to the room and then remembered Patricia locked upstairs alone too and decided to see if Eric had headed there. As they got back inside the room, he grabbed a sealed bottle and some mince pies.

‘What are you doing?’ asked Kailey.

‘I am taking these to the Foxs, I will be straight back down, just hide in here until I get back.’

‘Don’t be stupid, I’ll come with you.’ She said.

‘No, what if Eric comes back whilst we’re gone. I will be four minutes tops, and just hide under the sofa or something and stay there unless it’s me or Eric that comes back in.’ Robbie said.

Surprisingly she acquiesced easily with a short nod. Maybe running around the hotel wasn't a clever idea and she knew it. With that Robbie left the room.

'It's no use, I can't find a thing.' Katie said with exasperation, 'there could be twenty doors down here but we won't find them like this.'

'Ok, shall we head back to the door? We can just try shouting and hopefully the right person will hear us.' Eric replied. He shuffled in the dark, but was unsure as to which direction the door was. There was no light coming from below the door and it was still completely black in front of his eyes. 'I'm not sure which direction we're going in but let's feel around from the bottom of the steps.' He said clasping Katie's hand.

'Do you think everyone is ok upstairs?' Katie asked.

'I hope so, I hope Robbie has enough wits about him to stay safe and my auntie is locked away in her room.'

'Will she be safe there? She was the one who seemed to be the target.'

'Well only me and Robbie know she is there and she has locked and barricaded herself in.' Eric replied.

'What do you think is happening?' Katie asked as they continued fumbling along with arms out in front of them, waving looking for the bottom of the steps.

'Found it!' Eric said, as he felt the hard wooden frame acting as a bannister to the steps. 'You ok to climb a few steps? Then we can try and call for someone to open the door.'

'Yeah, I'll be ok, my wrist is throbbing though.' They steadily found the steps in front of them using their tentative kicks of their feet to find where each step rose before sitting down.

'We may as well listen out now, not much more we can do.' Eric said. Katie didn't reply but she gave his hand a soft squeeze.

'Answering your question, I really don't know what is going on or why. If I had some kind of reason as to why anyone at this hotel would hurt my auntie, I could guess who it could be.'

'I haven't a clue either, it doesn't make any sense.'

'We thought it might have been George but he has no keys so it he can't be hiding anywhere that one of us wouldn't have seen him.' Eric said.

'He wouldn't anyway, he is a lovely man and seems to worship the ground your auntie walks on.' Katie said, 'but he's the only one who is old enough to know your auntie and Robert.'

'What about Mr Fox? How old do you reckon he is?' Eric asked.

'Not that old, well he doesn't look it anyway and I'm sure Patricia doesn't recognise him.'

'Then again he wants to buy the hotel?' Eric said, sounding desperate to create a theory.

'Nice old school murder motive, but I don't see it happening, to be honest.'

'No, I guess you're right. Did you see who pushed you at all?' Eric enquired.

'No nothing just the hand in the back. I don't know if they thought they had killed me or not but it definitely wasn't an accident.' She said.

'Any ideas who might have wanted to hurt you?' Eric asked. He was finding it hard to frame the questions as he couldn't see or read Katie's facial expressions in her responses because of the dark.

'Not a clue.' She said softly, 'I mean I have nothing to do with Patricia outside of this hotel. So maybe they confused me with her?

Or maybe it's just a madman.' She said with an air of relinquish in her voice.

'Well me and Robbie thought that because we all knew Robert was murdered that maybe the killer would be backed into a corner and start killing everyone they could.' Eric said and he received no reply from Katie, 'kind of morbid, I know, but we were just trying to cover all bases.'

'Well I hope that isn't the case or it doesn't bode well for everyone upstairs.' Katie replied. They sat in silence for a while, Eric used the time to listen if he could hear anyone in the kitchen, he presumed Katie was doing the same. He sat back on his step.

'Why did you say you were calling your boyfriend before when we had no signal anywhere?' Eric asked. He knew it was a risky question as whilst he had felt like Katie was on his side, she could still be a suspect and picking holes in her character might not be the safest way forward. Fortunately, she laughed in response.

'Calm down Sherlock, nothing sinister there, I was actually trying to make a phone call but I knew we had no signal at that point but I was also politely excusing myself.'

'What do you mean?' Eric asked.

‘I was excusing myself from you two’s ogling eyes.’ Eric felt his face blush in the darkness, and felt that Katie would be able to see it even through the darkness. ‘Don’t worry Romeo, no need to be embarrassed, I actually have a long term girlfriend. And I was genuinely trying to call her. She must be so worried.’ Katie sadness came through on her final remark.

‘Don’t worry, we’ll get out of this and then you can do Christmas all over again with her when you get out of here.’ He heard Katie laugh again at this comment.

‘Sorry, I am still laughing at you. Was I on your *maybe* list for the murder? Didn’t me getting pushed down here spoil that theory?’ She laughed again.

‘Not at all, you could have faked the fall and the scream.’ Eric said defiantly in reply, and then both laughed. ‘Fine smart alec, who do you think is our chief suspect?’ Eric asked.

‘Maybe Brian? Don’t ask me what his motive would be as I don’t have a clue but he’s reserved yet intelligent and I’ve seen enough TV thrillers to know that’s a sign. Plus I guess I thought he had gone to the kitchen even though I never saw him, so he seemed like the person who was most likely to have pushed me.’ She said, ‘trust me, whilst I was down here alone, I ran through everyone who could have pushed me, and yes you were on that list too.'

'How very kind of you. I hate to break it to you, but apart from me, my auntie, and Robbie, I can't account for any of the guests when we heard you scream, so it could have been anyone.' Eric said in reply. 'Let's run through the guests. I guess we have nothing better to do in the meantime.' He said.

Robbie had checked on Patricia, and despite her overly cautious response to Robbie being alone, he soon found out that Eric wasn't with her so he left her locked in her room, and then headed down to the Fox's room. He didn't want to scare them especially after how wary Patricia had been with him so he was going to be as jovial as possible, worse comes to worst, he would just leave the drink and mince pies outside the door and head back down to Kailey. He arrived at their room and rattled the door, he heard the movement in the room, obviously getting off the beds and muffled footsteps approaching the door.

'Is that you?' He heard Mrs Fox's voice on the other side of the door call out.

‘Don’t worry, it’s just me Robbie, no need to open up, I just brought you up some mince pies and a bottle brandy, I thought you might need it after what happened.’ He called through the door.

‘That’s very kind of you, thank you.’ He heard the muffled voice come back from inside the room. ‘You can leave them outside and I’ll collect them soon. Thank you Robbie.’

‘No problem.’ He put the things down on the carpet outside their room, and left them to it. He felt like he had done a kind deed and there was no reason to see them and he’d feel safer leaving the empty corridors. He headed back downstairs, he encountered nobody on the stairs or in the main reception as he headed towards the main room with the fire. He assumed they must have all congregated in there, either that are they had taken a queue from the Fox family and headed to their own rooms. Robbie was tempted to do the same but without knowing where that third set of keys was, he wasn’t sure how safe being in his room was. He pushed open the door and walked into the main room, hoping to find Eric sat there but he was soon disappointed as he was met only with the blank stare of Brian sat by the fire. He looked around the room but could see no sign of Kailey either.

‘Evening.’ Brian said dryly.

‘Hello. Nobody else around?’ Robbie asked as he walked into the room. Brian held up his hand and showed Robbie the room with his hand sardonically. Robbie moved and sat down opposite Brian, keeping an eye on him.

‘You not heading to your room?’ Robbie asked.

‘Didn’t see much point with everything that is going on, one of you will only come and disturb me so I thought I would wait it out here.’ Brian sat back and stretched in his chair. Robbie had little to add to this comment but now was worried about Kailey as well as Eric.

‘You didn’t happen to see Kailey, when you came in here?’ he asked. Brian shook his head, but then saw that Robbie wanted him to elaborate.

‘There was nobody here when I came in about five minutes ago, I thought about heading to my room but I saw the fire and I presumed somebody had lit it and was planning to come back here.’ He looked at Robbie, ‘I assume now, that that was you.’ Robbie said nothing and the room returned to silence, the prickle of the fire burning away.

‘What do you make of all this?’ Robbie asked tentatively. He didn’t particularly feel like broaching the subject but the room was awkwardly quiet, maybe less so for Brian who seemed content by the fire, but Robbie felt he needed to talk to stop his mind racing.

‘About what?’ Brian said with a smile.

‘The murder, and whatever is going on in this hotel. You know the Foxs found a body in the snow?’

‘Quite the little detective aren’t you? You want to be careful asking so many questions.’ With that comment, the old grandfather clock in the room chimed 12 times.

CHAPTER 7 - CHRISTMAS DAY

After working their way through the guests, with nothing to form any type of conclusion bar their personalised judgements on each guest's characteristics, Eric and Katie sat in silence. None of the guests appeared to have any kind of motive, and the sale of the hotel seemed implausible and unlikely as any motive. Would Mr Fox bring his whole family to commit a murder over Christmas? Surely a hired hit man would do the job in such circumstances, Katie had said. Eric was about to mention the perfume but then he thought about how Katie could still be a suspect, he felt like it was a vital clue but he was still withholding it from Katie.

'I need to tell you something.' She said breaking the silence and Eric's internal weighing up of the situation.

'What's that?'

'Well I think I may have made it all a little more complicated.' She said

'Made what more complicated?' Eric asked curiously.

'Robbie, when he was attacked, hit over the head. It was me.'

'You? But why? What do you mean?' Eric felt his hands clamming, he wasn't sure if this was the beginning of some form of confession but he couldn't see anything in the dark so didn't know how to react.

'It's not what you think, I didn't mean to. I know that sounds stupid, but I didn't see who it was until the last second and I was scared.' She said, 'I'm really sorry, for a horrible second, I thought I had killed him but I have never hit someone over the head before, I didn't know how hard I had hit him.'

'You hit him all right, but I don't understand why. Why were you there hiding and what made you want to hit whoever was there?' Eric asked.

‘I went up to get the note, the one that Robert wrote.’ She replied.

‘Did you get it?’ Eric asked.

‘Yes, I’ve hidden it in my room. I went up because I thought it was evidence that something had happened and I thought if the killer found out they might try and retrieve it. I had just picked it up when I heard the door go, and my imagination and the nerves of being there, and with the dead body, I just panicked. I grabbed the paperweight thing and just hid behind the door. I didn’t want to hit anyone but I had convinced myself that it was the killer and if they found me there alone, they’d attack me too.’ She paused for a second, ‘I couldn’t believe it when it was Robbie. I thought I’d killed him but he rolled himself over so I ran downstairs and put the paperweight is his coat pocket as I was just not thinking. For a while I thought you and Robbie were up to something, but it didn’t make any sense so I gave you both the benefit of the doubt.’

‘Gee thanks.’ He laughed, ‘anyway, I didn’t come out of it badly, you might owe Robbie an apology later though.’

‘I know, I feel terrible, but I didn’t want to say anything, and then everyone was saying Robbie was attacked by the murderer, so I just stayed quiet.’ She said.

'Don't worry, hopefully this will be sorted out soon and Robbie won't hold a grudge for long.' Eric sat thinking for a second, 'it does mean that I have another suspect even if I can cross you of my list.'

'Who do you mean? Another suspect?' she asked.

'Hold on, I can hear someone in the kitchen.' Eric listened and Katie went quiet, the unmistakeable sound of footsteps in the kitchen.

Robbie stared at Brian who continued to stare at him. The fire crackling behind Brian had given his features an ominous shade with shadows which danced across his face.

'What do you mean?' Robbie asked.

'Well from somebody who was cracked over the head earlier, I would have thought you'd refrain from asking all sorts of questions. The killer might not make a mistake next time.' Brian said. Robbie felt himself squirming uncomfortably in his seat.

'Just mildly curious, and I'd like to get to the killer before they get to me.' Brian nodded and stared at Robbie.

'It's your funeral I guess. I'm trying to keep as far away and as safe as possible. I recommend you do the same.' Brian said, but his intensity had died and Robbie relaxed.

‘I’ll bear it in mind.’ Robbie replied. Then ignored Brian’s advice, he got up and poured himself a drink, coming to sit down in the chair where Robert had initially had a turn at the start of his stay in the hotel.

‘Swapping seats? Brian asked.

‘This is where Robert went a little weird just before he died. So I’m guessing he was poisoned here or something set him off.’

‘I thought he was drunk? Anyway that’s what Katie told me.’ Brian said.

‘Maybe, but he looked like he’d had the fright of his life, which at the time seemed like he’d had too many to drink, but maybe that wasn’t the case.’ Robbie looked around the room from the chair, attempting to remember where all the guests were, he could hardly remember who was present. He knew Brian hadn’t been there but he couldn’t remember the rest.

‘Is that the extent of your detective skills? Sitting in the chair and looking around?’ Brian laughed to himself. ‘I don’t think our killer need worry too much.’ Robbie rolled his eyes at the chuckling Brian and continued trying to think about who had been in the room. Something had set off Robert at the moment but he wasn’t sure who

or what or how, they had done it. Brian got up from his seat. Robbie watched him warily.
'I'm getting some food.' He said as he headed to the door. 'I'll be right back anyway.' He pulled open the door and Robbie looked at him as Brian stood there. Then he looked passed him. The chair had a direct line of sight to the reception desk. It came back to Robbie, Robert had taken a turn as Katie walked in, because at first, he had thought it was Katie who had triggered something in Robert but it wasn't Katie who had shocked Robert, he was looking past her and at the reception. Then Brian was joined by someone beside him. Brian turned in time to see Joe stood directly in front of him but he as too late as the knife plunged into Brian's stomach as he let out a cry, and fell backwards back into the room. He cradled himself on the floor, pushing his way back from Joe who was still holding the knife. Robbie jumped out of his chair and backed away, looking around for something to defend himself with but could see nothing by the fire. Joe stepped into the room and closed the door.

Eric and Katie listened at the door, half wondering who was in the kitchen or whether to shout out for help.
'What should we do?' Eric asked.

‘Well we can’t stay here forever.’ Katie replied, and she banged on the door, ‘Help!’ She shouted. Deciding so quickly and then acting upon her decision surprised Eric but it was too late to complain now she he shouted out too.

‘In here, please open the door!’ They stopped and both listened and the person who was in the kitchen had stopped, obviously surprised.

‘We’re in here, we’ve been locked in please open the door.’ Katie said. They could almost hear the trepidation in the silence of whoever was in the kitchen but it then relented as they heard the footsteps walk towards the door, and then a soft voice.

‘Who is it?’ Stephanie Fox said.

‘Stephanie, it’s me Katie, and I’m with Eric, somebody has locked us down here but we need to get out. Can you open the door?’

Stephanie must have believed the desperation in Katie’s voice as they heard the door handle and then the shove of the door. The light burnt their eyes at first until they adjusted to the kitchen lights. They climbed out of the stairwell.

‘Oh God, Stephanie, thank you.’ Katie said, ‘what are you doing down here alone anyway?’

'My parents are asleep, I came down as I'm hungry, I haven't eaten since this morning. Your friend brought us some mince pies, but I can't stand them.' She said looking at Eric.

'It's ok. Stay with us if you want, but let's go check everyone is ok.' Eric said closing the door and moving past the other two.

They arrived at the main lounge and quickly came across the commotion. Upon entering, Joe had whirled around from where he stood next to Robbie with the knife in his hand. Brian was on the floor and clutching his right side of his stomach and looking very pale.

'What are you doing Joe?' Katie asked pleadingly. Joe looked at Katie, with anger in his eyes. He was still edging towards Robbie who was trying to back away from, 'just put the knife down.'

'I didn't want this to happen, if you had all just let me do what needed to be done.' Joe said in reply. He kept his eyes on Robbie, but kept looking at the party who had entered the room, looking worried that they might rush him.

'What do you mean, I've done nothing wrong.' Robbie said trying to squeeze past the sofa by the fire to get behind it, keeping his eyes locked on Joe's knife.

‘No you might not have done, but with you all sniffing around, I’m going to have to stop you all. If you had just let me leave and this goddamned snow hadn’t come down, we wouldn’t be here.’ Joe said still walking slowly towards Robbie. Eric had told Stephanie to go up to her room and alert her parents but to then stay in her room, and she had slipped back out of the room, whilst Eric rolled up one of the throws from the chair nearest him and crouched down next to Brian, telling him to hold it firmly against the wound. Brian had nodded back to him so that alleviated Eric’s worry that Brian had been severely injured, nobody knew how long it would be until any emergency services would get up here so a minor wound could spell trouble.

‘How can it have been you, you were with Eric when I was attacked.’ Robbie pleaded.

‘That wasn’t me you idiot, I wouldn’t have left you alive if I had had the chance. Problem is you all keep going around together in groups so I never got to make a move. I knew when you started doing your Hardy boys act that it was time that I had to do something. I wanted to lock you in your rooms but then the keys kept on going missing.’

Joe said, as he finished he swiped forward at Robbie who shimmied backwards, almost falling backwards into the Christmas tree.
'But Joe, why are you doing all this?' Katie asked, looking around the room for something she could attack Joe with, seeing nothing, she decided that keeping him talking was their best strategy. Maybe they could lock him in here if they managed to get everybody out the room.
'It has nothing to with any of you, just Patricia, Robert, and George, none of you needed to get involved but you all started asking questions.' Joe said looking at Katie.
'But what did they do?' Eric asked.
'Stop with questions, didn't you hear him?' Robbie said and he laughed to himself. Joe quickly turned back on Robbie advancing towards him. 'Sorry I couldn't resist.' He squirmed away from the wall and towards Katie and Eric. The three of them stood with their backs to the wall. If they could manage to get Brian out the room, they could shut Joe inside. No guarantee he wouldn't break a window but they would be safer for a while, Eric thought. Joe stood with the knife out in front of him, he wouldn't be able to overpower them if they all rushed him but they probably wouldn't all make it

out of the scuffle without serious injuries so they stood staring Joe down.

Katie asked again pleadingly. It seemed to be touching a nerve with Joe, and Eric remembered that she had told him in the kitchen cellar that Joe was one of the good guys in the hotel, so the hurt in her voice sounded authentic and most probably genuine. Joe breathed a heavy sigh.

'Recall the photo, I kindly provided Patricia with or her school year? And how she egregiously could not recall much about Gerald, apart from how Robert had seen him a few times before his death and he was so *terribly depressed after his death*?' he mockingly sounded out the last of the sentence. 'Gerald was my father.' Joe looked around the room but the blank faces received his look and he rolled his eyes, now using his knife with each mannerism floating the object about in front of him. 'Obviously, you aren't the detectives I thought you were, or Patricia has let on less than I thought she would have under the circumstances.' Joe looked directly at Eric when he said this. 'Then again penance for her sins would be fitting with the death of a family member.' He said smiling and continuing to hold Eric's gaze. 'Fine! I'll do the work for you, as there is nobody to come and save the day, I might as well be frank before I vacate the vicinity. My father was bullied at your aunt's school whilst she was headmaster. And when I say bullied, I don't mean a few bad names, it changed his life, and everything after that school was different for him. You see I didn't know any of this growing up, my father turned his life around, settled down with a job, got married and had a family. But as usual things like this don't stay dead forever, Robert decided it was time to make amends for what had happened and came to visit my father but all it did was bring it all back, all of it. You see you hear about bullying but unless it happens to you, you don't know how it consumes you; well it came back and consumed my father. He lost his job, withdrew from our family, he stopped talking to us until eventually he decided to end it all, in our family home too. I was fiftenn, and then mother started drinking as she couldn't cope, so Robert's "terrible depression" is swatted away whilst my family was ruined because he thought he could make forty years or misery disappear with an apology.' Joe stopped and looked at them all, 'you see, sometimes people deserve what's coming to them.'

‘Robert didn’t deserve to die; your father wouldn’t have wanted that.’ Eric said.
‘How would you know?!?!’ Joe shouted at Eric, anger flaring in his eyes again, ‘you don’t know a thing, and yes my father did want all that, he wanted them all to pay for had happened, I heard them words leave his lips. I wasn’t going to let these people spoil somebody’s life and then go on about their normal life was I? First one was the hardest, I had to track down Mehmet Binks, find out when and how I could make his death look like an accident. I thought about hitting him in my car but I didn’t want to be implicated, he was just the first. So after finding out he and his family went on family ski holidays, I taught myself to ski, I hate skiing but it was worth it when I got to make sure that old fart crashed straight off course into trees. A year of skiing all for ten seconds of action but a lifetime of satisfaction.’ Joe smiled to himself.
‘But what about his family? You’re just as bad as them.’ Katie said.
‘I am not, and I never will be, what happened to them happened was seconds in a lifetime of happiness, my family has slowly been dying from the day my father left school. Raymond Williams was easy,

followed the man hiking, he even went by himself so was no need to plan anything apart from pushing him off a steep cliff. They didn't even find him for a few weeks, so at least his family felt the kind of pain I have for a while.' He said smiling to himself. 'Then the coup de grace, the thing is, this Christmas has been tied up nicely in a bow for me, I didn't even know Robert was coming. When I found out that stupid oaf George from the school worked here as well as your aunt, it was too good to be true, and then getting a job here. The obnoxious idiots didn't have an idea who I was.'

'But why do they have to die? What have they got to do with it? You can't blame the whole school.' Eric said.

'No I can't but any blame at their feet is justified, they both knew what was going on, they both turned a blind eye. They were supposed to be the adults, the people to stop what was going on, but they let it happen. My only regret is that I let them live so long. George was fun, I took my time, making sure he knew he was being watched, like watching prey, and I think he knew too. Then low and behold, I found out that the last of my targets was coming to stay over Christmas. I would finally have my vengeance. It was then I decided that I would travel to Brazil and live in the knowledge that what I had done was right.' Joe moved a step closer to the three of them and Brian was still curled up on the floor holding the blanket to his midriff. 'I decided I would poison them both, nice and easy in their sleep and then slip away. But the old fool saw me didn't he? He must have recognised me from all those years before visiting my father. Then had that ridiculous scene stumbling to his room, luckily I had already left the poison in his drink upstairs and the idiot drank it, but I knew he had recognised me. So you see ladies and gentleman, that now only your aunt remains. I had planned to just attack her but she has done well in keeping somebody with her at all times, but then I decided with the snow, if I kill all of you, and then I can let her know exactly what I think of her and there will be nobody to stop me.'

'You lunatic.' Brian spat out his words and winced.

'Quite the contrary my friend, I care little for getting away with murder but I do plan to murder all of you before getting away from punishment. Whilst at first I hated the snow, I now see how it is keeping you all here rather conveniently so I can continue with what I started. Rather annoyingly, some of you seem harder to kill than others.' He looked at Katie. 'Yes yes Katie, it was your old friend who pushed you down the stairs.' The mania in Joe's voice seemed to be rising and Eric was worried that Joe was going to go into a frenzy at any time. It was at that point he saw the long leg of Kailey slowly stepping out from behind the Christmas tree. He didn't care how or why Kailey was there but he knew he had to keep Joe occupied otherwise there wouldn't be anything stopping him using that knife on Kailey.

'What your dad and your family has gone through is terrible, but this won't make amends for any of that.' Eric said pleadingly, and he kept his eyes on Joe, using his peripheral vision to see Kailey creep from behind the tree until see was standing unprotected. One creak in her footsteps and Joe would turn on her.

'Oh yes it will make amends. You have watched too many TV programmes, I feel no remorse for any of these people, and you are unfortunate but ultimately you have to die too as I don't intend on spending the rest of my life in a prison. You see, when I killed Mehmet, I didn't feel sad, I didn't have nightmares or flashbacks, I felt relief, a warmth coming over me every night, and that satisfaction gets better with every piece of justice I deal out.' Kailey took a step towards Joe.

‘But this isn’t justice.’ Katie said.

‘No maybe not for you Katie, but sacrifices are to be made in the name of justice. Anyway, enough of this prattle, I still have a den of Foxes upstairs waiting for me after you lot. And that whining Kailey.’ She took another step forward at this, and he turned but only in time to see Kailey grab the paperweight from where Eric had placed it on the bookshelf, and before he could whirl his arm around with the knife he was holding, she had crashed it square on his forehead. Joe collapsed to the floor like a mannequin with its strings cut.

‘Good shot!’ Robbie let out, as the others rushed forward. Katie grabbed the knife and Eric sat on top of Joe. ‘That paperweight is definitely coming home with me now!’ Robbie exclaimed.

CHAPTER 8 - BOXING DAY

After ensuring that Joe was tied up and seeing to Brian as best they could. The rest of the guests were rounded up and they kept vigil over Joe throughout Christmas Day. He had been animated when he first awoke but then his situation seemed to dawn on him and he spent most the day in what seemed like a contemplative silence. Whilst the tone of the room was not jovial, a sense of relief spread through the guests in the knowledge that they were safe and the element of distrust dissipated. The snow began to melt throughout Christmas Day but none of them had noticed due to their tired states and due to spending the full day together in the main room by the fire. They were jolted back to reality with the sound of Christmas carols floating in the air on Boxing Day morning. They were in for a surprise when a gushing Fox family burst out of the hotel to greet the carollers. The road at the bottom had been cleared on Christmas Day so traffic was moving, and eventually as the snow melted away, the path Eric and Robbie had made through the snow on their way to Eve Manor had been accessible for the carol singers to make their way to the hotel. Eric and Robbie watched as each of the hotel's inhabitants departed. Brian was taking away in an ambulance and Joe soon followed in a police car. The police came and went and filled the hotel with people from all their departments looking into what had happened over the festive stay at the hotel. The Fox family then departed with permission before Kailey also left. Kailey took the paperweight, and whilst Robbie had wanted it, he decided she deserved it, plus she wanted to make it centrepiece of her internet blog on what had happened. She was pleased to find that the local buzz had already increased her web presence. Katie stayed for a while as her girlfriend had to make the journey to come and collect her and then too had gone.

‘Auntie why don’t you come spend some time with us? It’s not like you’ve managed to have a Merry Christmas.’ Eric said, as he and Robbie brought their bags down to the hotel reception. The police had already forewarned them that they would need to speak to them again at some point soon to clarify all the details of Joe.

‘Honestly Eric, I am fine, I’m tougher than I look. Anyway, I think if I handle this media attention correctly, I could get rid of this place. Not sure Mr and Mrs Fox will be following up on their interest.’ She said with a smile.

‘Ok then Auntie, well the offer is there.’ Eric said and gave his aunt a hug. Patricia looked at Robbie and prepared to offer a hand, before Robbie leaned in and hugged her.

‘Great Christmas.’ He said and she smiled as she hugged him back. The two of them left, and trudged away from the hotel, a flurry of vehicles and people had completely cleared the snow from the drive.

‘Wonder where the car is? They can’t have just left it in the road.’ Eric said, feeling worried they were walking without anywhere to actually go.

‘Suppose we can go to the pub anyway.’ Robbie suggested. ‘Plus! The drinks on are on me.’ Eric looked surprisingly at Robbie. ‘No need to look at me like that, I regularly buy drinks. My White Christmas bet came off.' He said smiling, 'just checked my betting account.'

'How much have we made?' Eric asked.

'We? I have made £9.32' He answered.

'Blimey mate, better quit our jobs.' Eric laughed, 'how much did you put on?'

'Just a couple of quid. I'm not made of money. Anyway, it'll get us a pint and an half each.' Robbie said.

'Sounds perfect mate. Merry Christmas.'

11665873R00120

Printed in Great Britain
by Amazon